Game Plan for Disaster

Frank and Joe waited until they were sure Ace had left the building. Then they dashed down to the front door. Joe peeked through the window. "He's going toward Main Street and moving quickly."

The brothers crept out the entrance and ran silently after the athlete. They stayed about twenty-five yards behind, keeping to the shadows and darting from tree to tree.

Some distance ahead, a car's parking lights flicked on. As the unsuspecting Ace started across the street the automobile glided forward, moving slowly with a low hum. Suddenly, the headlights flashed on, and the vehicle roared ahead at top speed. The startled student stood paralyzed as the car headed straight for him!

The Hardy Boys Mystery Stories

#59 Night of the Werewolf
#60 Mystery of the Samurai Sword
#61 The Pentagon Spy
#62 The Apeman's Secret
#63 The Mummy Case
#64 Mystery of Smugglers Cove
#65 The Stone Idol
#66 The Vanishing Thieves
#67 The Outlaw's Silver
#68 Deadly Chase
#69 The Four-headed Dragon
#70 The Infinity Clue
#71 Track of the Zombie
#72 The Voodoo Plot
#73 The Billion Dollar Ransom
#74 Tic-Tac-Terror
#75 Trapped at Sea
#76 Game Plan for Disaster
#77 The Crimson Flame
#78 Cave-In!
#79 Sky Sabotage
#80 The Roaring River Mystery
#81 The Demon's Den
#82 The Blackwing Puzzle
#83 The Swamp Monster
#84 Revenge of the Desert Phantom
#85 The Skyfire Puzzle
#86 The Mystery of the Silver Star

Available from MINSTREL Books

76

The HARDY BOYS®

GAME PLAN FOR DISASTER

FRANKLIN W. DIXON

A MINSTREL™ BOOK

PUBLISHED BY POCKET BOOKS

A Minstrel Book published by
POCKET BOOKS, a division of Simon & Schuster, Inc.,
1230 Avenue of the Americas, New York, N.Y. 10020

ISBN: 0-671-64288-X

Produced by Mega-Books of New York, Inc.

First Minstrel Books printing October, 1987

10 9 8 7 6 5 4 3 2 1

Contents

1	*Strange Accidents*	1
2	*Robbie's Trouble*	10
3	*The Shocked Professor*	22
4	*Danger in the Dark*	34
5	*No Comment*	46
6	*Kidnapped!*	56
7	*The Eavesdropper*	64
8	*Dismissed*	72
9	*The Gold Bug*	81
10	*Ace Runs Away*	90
11	*Lost in a Blizzard*	99
12	*Trapped!*	105
13	*Lucky Rescue*	116
14	*Carol Is Accused*	130
15	*Fire!*	144
16	*No Charge*	153
17	*Another Arrow*	160
18	*The Clincher*	171
19	*Chaos*	179
20	*Capture*	186

GAME PLAN
FOR DISASTER

1 Strange Accidents

Dr. Angelo Catello, president of State University, was suffering from a severe case of nerves. His usually placid face was marked by a deep frown. He paced his office, sat down abruptly, tapped his fingers on his desk for a few moments, and then rose to pace again.

"We've had trouble on campus, Mr. Hardy," he said. "Lots of trouble!"

The detective, who sat on a couch between his teenage sons Frank and Joe, looked at him questioningly. "What kind of trouble, sir?"

"You've heard of Kevin Harrington, otherwise known as Ace Harrington?"

"State's star quarterback?" dark-haired Frank blurted out. "Sure we have!"

1

Mr. Hardy smiled. "I think we've all heard of the great all-American."

"Good. And you're aware, I suppose, that State is playing Northern University in our final game, which has been heralded as a contest for the national championship."

The detective nodded.

"I don't believe that any educational institution should overemphasize athletics, but, on the other hand, I think it must be an essential part of the curriculum. So we are most proud that our football team has been rated so high in the polls.

"We are also very proud of Ace Harrington. He's overcome many problems. He comes from a poverty-stricken area, his mother died four years ago, and his father has been quite ill, and living in a nursing home."

"We read about that in the papers," blond, seventeen-year-old Joe spoke up. "He has a younger brother, too, who's in a foster home."

"That's right," Dr. Catello confirmed. "Now, despite his bad fortune, Ace is doing very well here. He's popular on campus, and not for his athletic prowess alone. He has a warm personality and has played an important part in campus and senior class projects. But most of all, he's a brilliant student."

2

"A real brain," Frank added. "The article said he's been on the deans list since he was a freshman."

"That's right," the college president stated. "Professor Overton, his faculty adviser, says that Harrington is the smartest student in physics he's ever taught. Ace has an excellent chance to get a Rhodes Scholarship for graduate work in England. He also, I understand, will be offered a king's ransom to play professional football."

"But how does all this figure in your problem?" Mr. Hardy came to the point.

The college president sighed. "Strange things have happened for which we have no explanation. Several times in the past two weeks, Harrington has barely escaped serious injury in a number of mysterious accidents."

"Which perhaps weren't accidents at all?" Frank asked.

"That's my feeling," Dr. Catello replied. "For instance, a heavy flowerpot fell from a third-story window, missing Harrington by inches. Another time a big box of sand was placed in front of his door at night. He tripped over it, but fortunately was not badly hurt. A few days ago, someone stole a poisonous snake—a pit viper—from the zoology department and put it

3

in Harrington's athletic locker."

"Did it bite him?" Mr. Hardy asked.

"It did, but it was harmless. The fangs had been removed by the zoology department. There were no clues, not even a fingerprint. To this day, no one knows how the locker was broken into."

"Does Ace have an idea who might be doing this to him?" Frank inquired.

"That's the strangest part," Catello said. "I had him in here yesterday and asked him the same question. He was very reticent about it all. I asked him why he didn't report even one attempt on his life, why they were reported by others. He replied that they were only accidents. He explained the snake away by saying it must have been a prank by a fellow student who knew the viper had been defanged."

"What precisely do you wish us to do?" Mr. Hardy asked.

"To guard Harrington without being too obvious and to apprehend the vicious character behind these attacks!" Dr. Catello took off his glasses and looked directly at Fenton Hardy. "I realize that's a pretty tall order, but I'm afraid for the youth. Believe me when I say that my concern is not because of the Northern game, but because I truly admire Harrington."

4

"I understand," Mr. Hardy said. "I brought Frank and Joe. They have a week off from school because of a teachers' convention. You see, my assistant and I are engaged in a case in Texas that requires our immediate attention. But my sons can adequately guard Ace and, hopefully, catch the person who is trying to hurt him."

The college president looked dubious. "They seem young." He glanced at the boys. "With all due apologies."

"That's an advantage," the detective pointed out. "They will blend into the student body easily enough while Sam Radley and I would stick out like sore thumbs."

Dr. Catello hesitated. "Still . . ."

"I see you have doubts," Mr. Hardy said. "I'm surprised you haven't heard of the fine work my sons have done, but no offense is taken. I can provide you with a list of qualified detective agencies run by friends of mine in whom I have absolute trust."

He half-rose, but Dr. Catello waved him to sit again. "Mrs. Catello tells me that sometimes I am too cautious, that I look too long before I leap. I have called upon you to come here because I needed an expert in the field of detection. You have given me certain advice—

namely that your two sons can handle this case—and I certainly should take it. Suppose I find living quarters for Frank and Joe somewhere in the vicinity of Harrington's room? Pardon me a moment."

He phoned the college office in charge of dormitories and spoke for a minute, then he put the receiver down. "The student who lives opposite Harrington's room has had a very serious operation and has been sent home to recuperate for the remainder of the semester. His room will be free. Frank and Joe can pick up the key in the dormitory office."

"That will be convenient," Fenton Hardy said.

The Hardys stood up and shook hands with President Catello. "If you can get to the bottom of this mystery," the administrator said, "the university will be eternally grateful."

The three Hardys strolled back to the campus parking lot, talking about the case and the procedures the boys should follow.

They were approaching their car when Mr. Hardy stopped. "Isn't that Ace Harrington getting out of that sedan over there?"

Frank and Joe followed his gaze. "It sure is," Joe said. "I'd know him anywhere after seeing his picture in the papers so often. What do you say we introduce ourselves and tell him we're going to be neighbors for a while?"

He started forward, but his father caught him by the arm. "Hold it," he said. "He doesn't look like he wants any casual conversation at the moment. Let's stay here and watch what happens."

Two men in the front seat of the car Ace had left stared straight ahead, as motionless as toy soldiers. The man in the back seat had his head out of the window and was obviously arguing with the football star. His gravelly voice floated across the parking lot. "You better play ball with us or else!"

Ace said something that the Hardys couldn't hear, but it infuriated the man. He snapped his fingers and the driver got out of the car, holding a small dark object in his right hand.

"That's a blackjack!" Mr. Hardy exclaimed. "Come on!"

Ace was backing away, his fists ready. The Hardys hurried toward the automobile, but the man in the back seat saw them coming. He snapped an order to his henchman with the blackjack, who immediately jumped back into the sedan, started the engine, and drove away toward the exit.

Ace had not seen his would-be rescuers. He

stared after the car with a mixture of fury and confusion. Then he turned on his heels and walked out of the parking lot in the opposite direction.

The Hardys stopped. "I know the man in the back seat," Mr. Hardy said. "He's Albert Camor—better known as 'Sureshot.' He's a notorious professional gambler who has been involved in some very shady deals. I wonder what Ace was doing in his car?"

No one had the answer to Mr. Hardy's question, and they discussed the mystery on the way back to Bayport. At home, the boys quickly packed, got into their own car, and returned to the college.

It was early evening when they pulled into the parking lot. Joe pointed and said, "Look at that!"

Barely hidden by bushes on the edge of the lot, a gigantic man was holding a young boy's arm in a vicious grip while slapping the youth at the same time.

Frank jammed on the brakes and he and Joe leaped out. As they approached, they heard the giant say, "You be there tonight, in the basement of Williams Hall at ten o'clock sharp, you hear, you dummy? Meeb wants you there."

"Cut that out!" Joe shouted.

The man and the boy both turned and stared at the Hardys for a long moment. Then the man released his grip on the youth and hurried off among the cars and into the dark, wooded area beyond.

2 Robbie's Trouble

The Hardys ran after him, but lost the stranger, who apparently knew his way around the campus. When they returned to the parking lot, the boy was gone, too.

"This is a crazy place," Joe said. "Where do you think the kid went?"

Frank shrugged. "I have no idea. Let's go and get our key." They went to the dormitory office, then found their room. It was comfortable, with two beds, a large window overlooking the campus, and walls lined with books.

"The fellow who lives here must be some reader," Joe said. "Or do you think he's just showing off?"

Frank laughed. "It would be an expensive way to show off. Anyway, these books are mostly about economics so he's probably majoring in that. Let's go over and introduce ourselves to Ace."

The door opposite proclaimed HARRINGTON in capital letters, but no one answered after they knocked several times.

"That's funny," Frank said as they went back to their room. "I thought I heard moving around in there."

"So did I."

"Let's try again later. Meanwhile, we should find out where Williams Hall is. If this bully is meeting the boy he hit earlier, I'd like to see what's going on."

"That's a good idea," Joe agreed.

The boys located Williams Hall on their way to the cafeteria, where they stopped to have dinner. Then, at ten o'clock, they staked out the building where the meeting was to take place. At first, they could see nothing, but soon they heard voices. Quietly, they traced the sounds to a basement window. A dim light within revealed three indistinct figures. Frank and Joe could make out the shadow of the big man who had bullied the boy earlier.

"It's good you came, Robbie," the huge man

said. "Otherwise, Mr. Meeb here might be very unhappy. And when he's unhappy, I'm unhappy. And when I'm unhappy, I take it out on the people that make him unhappy, understand?"

"Just don't squeeze my arm again," another shadow said.

"He only looks about nine or ten years old. I can't believe these guys," Joe whispered.

Meeb became more distinct as he moved nearer to the basement window that Joe and Frank were looking through. He was a very small man—smaller than Robbie—with a bowler hat and a checkered suit in a wide print.

"Leave him alone, Scrabby," he ordered in a squeaky voice. "Robbie is here and that is all that matters at the moment. You understand what you have to do, kid?"

"I know what you want me to do," the youth replied, "but I don't think I want to do it. It's bad, awfully bad."

"You let us worry about that, Robbie. That way you won't be punished for it."

"You want me to teach him another lesson?" Scrabby said. "Give him what I gave him this afternoon?"

Meeb held up a restraining hand. "That won't be necessary. Robbie's a sensible boy. He knows what will happen to his mother if he doesn't do as we say. Isn't that true, Robbie?"

The young man mumbled something.

"What did you say?" Meeb's voice was sharp this time. "Speak up or I'll have to show you how Scrabby can improve you."

"I said I will have to do it because of what you could do to my mother." Robbie was near hysteria.

"That's good," Meeb purred. "Now here is what you will put in its place." He handed a small package to the youth. "When you have it, bring it to the old house. Do you remember where it is?"

"Yes."

"All right. We'll be there every night at seven o'clock. Now I know you have to wait until the right moment, but we don't wish to wait *too* long. Suppose we give you four days. If you don't deliver by that time, we'll go for your mother. I guess I've covered it all. Did I miss anything, Scrabby?"

"That's all, Mr. Meeb." The giant cracked his knuckles ominously. "You remember what he said, kid."

The light went out and the voices faded away.

Frank touched Joe's arm and motioned him behind a large shrub near the front door, which was not far from the basement window.

"We'll wait here for them, then follow those guys," he suggested.

"There could be another exit," Joe cautioned. "Why don't I go around the building, just in case?"

"That's a good idea."

Joe left, but returned a few minutes later. "I saw a cellar door, but it was padlocked from the outside," he reported.

Frank frowned. "I wonder what's taking them so long?"

The boys waited ten minutes, then both went around the building. There was no sign of the men and the youth, and no lights were on anywhere.

"They vanished!" Frank complained. "I wonder how they got out?"

"Maybe there's a passageway to the next building in the basement," Joe suggested. "Too bad we don't know our way around here yet."

Frank nodded. "And I wish we had a few answers. Like who's this boy Robbie? What's he going to steal? Where and who is his mother?"

Joe sighed. "I guess we just have to wait and keep our eyes open for those characters. Do you think we should notify the police?"

"What would we be able to tell them?" Frank

challenged. "That we heard two guys named Meeb and Scrabby plan what appears to be a theft and that they forced a kid named Robbie to join in? That we have no idea what they're planning to steal, or where, or when?"

"It sounds feeble," Joe admitted.

"You bet," Frank grumbled. "Well, let's go back and see if Ace is in his room."

They were just passing the library when Frank glanced up the long stone stairway leading to the entrance. "That's a real impressive building," he commented, "the way it's sitting on that hill." He suddenly pointed. "Isn't that Ace Harrington who just came out?"

Joe narrowed his eyes to see better. "Yes, that's him."

"Let's wait here," Frank said. "We can introduce ourselves and walk with him back to the dorm."

Ace stopped for a moment to look up at the starless, dark sky. Then he started to descend the fifty or so steps. He had gone down three steps when a figure rose from behind a bush by the library door. Apparently, someone else was waiting for the star athlete. The figure approached swiftly with his hands out.

"Watch out, Ace!" Frank shouted. "Behind you!"

15

Ace started to turn his head, but he was too late. The next instant he was shoved violently forward. His feet left the concrete and he flew through the air. He fell on his side six steps down and then rolled to the next landing. There he lay perfectly still. Ace's assailant did not stop to see what injury he had inflicted on his victim. Instead, he hurried off the steps to the side and ran down the steep, grassy hill on a slant.

"Go get him, Joe!" Frank yelled as he started up the steps toward the young athlete. Joe was already in motion and pursuing the attacker, who was quickly disappearing into the darkness.

"What's going on?" A middle-aged, uniformed man called out. He had just arrived at the library building and was hurrying up the steps after Frank.

"Ace Harrington was attacked!" the Hardy boy replied.

"Oh, no!"

When the two reached the young football player, he was struggling to rise.

"Don't get up, Ace!" the older man cautioned, "until we get a doctor to look you over."

Harrington looked at him. "Oh, hello Pops." Don't worry, I'm not hurt badly. It's no worse than getting tackled hard."

"What happened, anyhow?" Pops asked.

"Some kid in a hurry happened to bump into me. It was just an accident."

The older man looked around. "Where is he?"

"Oh, he dashed off. He didn't even know he had knocked me down, I guess."

"He acted as if he did," Frank said dryly. "He was hiding in those bushes up there, sneaked up behind you with his arms out and then, after he had shoved you, he ran over on the grass and down the hill."

Ace stared at Frank. "Who are you?"

"Frank Hardy. My brother and I have been assigned to guard you."

"Oh, yeah, I got a note from Dr. Catello about you." The football player was on his feet by this time. "I realize he's worried about me, but he's exaggerated a bunch of little incidents into a huge plot. I don't need any nursemaids, so you can just forget it and go home!"

He went down the steps, still wobbly. The older man shook his head. "I've seen him like that on a football field. He gets hit hard and stands up for the next play. Coach Bradley had to practically sit on him to get him to take a little rest."

He put out his hand. "I'm John Walzak,

known around here as 'Pops.' I'm the head of the campus police. I heard this afternoon that you and your brother were coming. Any time you need help, just call on me."

Frank shook hands with Walzak. "Thank you. We probably will need help sometime." They heard a whistle from below and looked down. "That's my brother. He was chasing the guy who shoved Ace. Would you like to talk to him?"

"Sure. Any information will be useful for my report."

They walked down and Frank introduced Joe to the campus police chief.

"I'm glad to meet you, Mr. Walzak. You know, that guy looked heavy to me, and I thought I wouldn't have any trouble catching him. But he was fast. He was ahead of me and just disappeared."

"Hmm, he knows the campus, probably," Pops said. "It'll be like searching for a needle in a haystack, and we barely have a clue what the person looks like!"

"I know," Frank said, discouraged. "Well, we'd better try to catch up with Ace and talk some sense into him. Good night, Mr. Walzak."

"Good night, fellows, and good luck."

Ace was already in his room when the boys

reached the dorm. When they knocked, he opened the door a crack and peered out. "Oh, it's you," he said grumpily.

"We just want to talk with you, Ace," Frank said. "What's the harm in that?"

Slowly and reluctantly, the student came out. He shut the door quickly behind him.

"Look, I know you're trying to do your job," he said to them, "but really I don't need any guards. President Catello is a great guy, but he's blown some small, unrelated events into a big conspiracy."

"Like the attack tonight?" Joe said skeptically. "That guy was waiting for you. We saw him come out of the bushes and jump you. He wanted to injure you."

"Be reasonable, Ace," Frank pleaded. "If we don't tail you, someone else will. The university isn't going to let you alone while these 'accidents' continue to happen."

Ace rubbed his chin and studied both of them carefully. At last he said, "I guess it's okay. Only promise you won't pry into my personal life. When I close the door to my room, that's it until I come out again."

The boys looked at each other. Then Frank said, "We won't invade your privacy. After all, you have your studying to do."

The sports star grinned. "In that case, I'll go along with the deal." He shook hands with them. "Now I'll tell you what my life is like. I get up at six and run five miles. Then I take a long cold shower. I go to classes for most of the day, get out on the field at four, and practice until seven. Then I eat and usually study until eleven. You want to go through all that?"

Frank smiled. "A job is a job."

"Tomorrow's Sunday," Ace went on. "I'll have to study in the morning, then I have a physics lab."

"Isn't that unusual?" Joe asked.

"It is. But we had to cancel one, and everyone volunteered to make it up this Sunday. We also have football practice, which we usually don't on the weekend. But it's so close to the big game that we decided we'd better. So, will I see you tomorrow?"

"I'm not wild about running at six in the morning," Joe said, grimacing. "And I don't think I'll take the cold shower. But the rest is fine."

When the Hardys returned to their room, Joe said, "That bit about not prying into his personal life or not going into his room is kind of odd, isn't it?"

"It is," Frank agreed, "especially when we

20

wouldn't anyhow. But it's his right. Our responsibility ends at his doorstep."

"But is he safe even in his room?"

Frank bit his lip. "I hope so."

3 The Shocked Professor

Joe groaned when the alarm clock went off at quarter to six the next morning. Surprisingly, though, he found the five-mile run enjoyable. It was a beautiful fall day, cool and fresh. The three young men ran on a wooded trail through a small forest just off the campus. The leaves were still falling and provided a gold and brown carpet under their feet.

After their run, Ace disappeared into his room to study, while the Hardys read. After lunch, they all went to the physics laboratory. "This'll probably be boring for you," Ace said. "There's no lecture, everyone works on his own."

"In our line of work, you learn patience," Frank said. "Many times we have to just sit around and wait for something or someone."

"Well, be my guest."

But the next hour wasn't as boring as Ace had predicted.

Professor Overton walked over to Frank and Joe as soon as the roll had been taken. "You're the Hardys, aren't you?" He laughed at their surprised expressions. "Nothing happens on this campus that the entire faculty does not know within twenty-four hours. Welcome to our laboratory. Let me show you around." The tall, lanky professor took them on a guided tour. There was much that the boys didn't understand, especially the functions of brand-new instruments, but it was obvious that the genial instructor was an excellent teacher.

"This is an advanced laboratory group," he explained after they had finished and were sitting by his desk. "It is only open to students who have completed six semesters of physics and have B+ averages. So you can see what kind of company Ace is in. I am very proud of him. He's my prize student."

"He's pretty terrific as a football player, too," Joe broke in.

Overton made a face. "It's just a game. What

he does here is serious. He's got a fine future as a physicist. You know, everyone in this laboratory is involved in a special project. Ace is working in an area that is very near to my heart."

"What's that, sir?" Frank asked.

The teacher lowered his voice. "An inexpensive way to extract oil from shale. It has been done, you know, but costs a great deal. If I can discover a cheaper process, it will be a boon to the human race!"

"Have you been working on it for a long time?"

"Years and years," Overton half whispered. "I have devoted my every free moment to it—each weekday and weekend evening during the school year and my summer vacations as well." His eyes sparkled. "And I'll tell you a secret." They could barely hear him now. "I'm on the edge of success! Only a little more time and I'll be able to announce it to the world!"

"That's great!" Frank said.

Overton nodded. "Next weekend the International Society of Physicists is meeting right here at the university. I requested permission to read a paper on my research thus far."

"That's the weekend of the football game," Joe said. "Won't that interfere?"

"It will in a way," Overton said, "because our beloved president has invited the members of the society to attend the game. That means we won't really be able to begin till Sunday." His voice had taken on a slightly sneering tone, reflecting what he thought about college sports. Then he smiled. "The members of the society have been ignoring me for years, but they won't anymore, not after they hear what I have to say!"

He was so intent on his subject that he did not notice that Ace had walked up and was standing over him.

"Here's my work for today, Professor," the young man said, handing Overton a sheaf of papers.

"Thank you, Ace. I'll take a glance at it now, but I won't be able to give you my full reaction until next week."

"That's fine, sir." Ace looked at the Hardys. "I'm going to put away equipment and clean up. Then I'll be with you."

As the boys waited, they saw a strange reaction from Overton. He was casually reading Ace's report when he seemed to go into a kind of shock. His mouth fell open and his eyes flew to the top of the page again. He reread it to the very bottom. Then his hands started to tremble. He looked out of the window with a vacant stare.

"Is there anything wrong, Professor?" Frank cried.

Overton shook himself out of his trance and forced a smile. "No, no, nothing," he said.

Just then the buzzer sounded, marking the end of the lab session. Overton slipped out of his white coat and was putting on his tweed jacket when Ace returned and asked him one final question relating to his report. Overton answered it on the way to the main floor. He had not quite finished when they reached the small physics department office. "Ace, excuse me a second," he said. "I want to check my mail. I didn't have a chance yesterday." With that, he went inside.

A moment later, he rejoined the group, with an envelope in his hand. "Well, now we shall see," he said excitedly. He was so nervous that his fingers had difficulty opening the envelope. He pulled out a sheet and read it eagerly.

Suddenly, his already pale face fell and then contorted with fury. Without a word, he jammed the letter into his pocket and stomped away!

"Wow!" Ace said. "Something must have really shaken him up. I've never seen him like that."

"I guess he got bad news," Frank agreed. He had noticed the return address on the envelope.

It was the International Society of Physicists.

The Hardys and Ace started off toward the football stadium. "This might not be very exciting to you two," Ace said. "We're having light calisthenics, then we'll watch a videotape of Northern University's last game. No contact work."

"I'm sure we'll find something to be interested in," Frank said lightly.

"I'll be interested in everything," Joe exclaimed.

"Hey, Harrington." The raspy voice came from behind them. The three youths whirled since they all recognized the voice.

Sureshot Camor and his two henchmen were approaching. Ace's hands doubled into fists and he growled, "Stay right there!"

The newcomers halted.

"That's no way to be friendly, kid, no way at all," the gambler said. "I just wanted to say that I'm sorry we had our little altercation yesterday."

"Buzz off!"

Camor put out his hands, palms up, placatingly. "Now that's not being very polite. I just want to have a little chat. Let's go somewhere we can talk privately." He looked meaningfully at Frank and Joe.

Joe stepped forward impulsively. "We're not leaving."

"Stay out of this, Joe," Ace said softly, then turned back to Sureshot. "You get out of here or we'll get the campus police."

"Do it," the gambler said dryly. "They'll be interested to hear what we know. Anyway, they can't kick us off the college grounds. This is a *state* university, remember? It was paid for by taxpayers' money and belongs to the citizens. It's public property. And I'm breaking no law."

Ace took a step toward him. "Get out or—" he said threateningly.

"Did you forget that I'm protected, Ace?" Sureshot waved towards his tough henchmen.

"Well, he's got us to help him," Frank said, stepping beside Ace.

"Hold it!" Ace ordered. "This has gone too far. I'm losing my temper, which is foolish. Look, Camor, I've said all I'll ever say to you. Now I'm going to practice." He turned and walked off, followed by Frank and Joe.

Camor called out, "If you're in that game, it will be the last day you stay in this college and you know it, Harrington!"

"Who was that?" Frank asked, "and what does he mean by those threats?"

"None of your business!" the football star snapped. "Remember what I said about my privacy?"

"We also remember that you're being threatened," Frank said. "This guy's obviously blackmailing you and probably has something to do with those accidents—"

"I can't talk about it!" Ace said evenly. "Now don't waste your time badgering me." With that, he strode quickly to the stadium.

Frank and Joe sat in the stands, watching the team do push-ups. "What do you think Camor has on Ace?" Joe asked.

"I wish I knew!" Frank replied.

Later, they watched the videotape of the Northern University game from the back of the locker room. The coach pointed out the weaknesses and strengths of the rival's defenses and offenses. Finally, the team was dismissed. Ace left abruptly, and the Hardys had to run to catch up to him.

Another attempt at dinner to make Ace confide in them failed, and when they reached their hall, the young football player unlocked his door and turned to them. "Good night," he said gruffly and disappeared into his room, slamming the door.

The Hardys left their door slightly ajar, just enough to keep their eye on Ace's room. Frank was reading a book while Joe was watching TV when there was a small knock and a smiling face appeared in the opening. "Hello!"

"Come on in," Frank said, recognizing Robbie, the young boy who had been bullied by Scrabby. Joe rose and turned off the television.

Robbie stopped when he had taken two steps inside the room and gazed admiringly at the walls. "Wow!" he said. "Look at all those books! It must have taken you a pretty long time to read them."

Frank laughed. "We haven't read them. We're just using this room for a little while. I'm Frank Hardy and this is my brother, Joe. Sit down, won't you?"

"Thank you." Robbie sat on a bed. "I—saw you with Ace a little while ago, having dinner. Afterward I decided to follow you. My name is Robbie."

Frank's eyes met Joe's.

"We're glad to meet you, Robbie," Frank said.

Robbie pointed to the books again. "I really like books. Right now I'm reading *Treasure Island*. It's one of my mother's favorites."

"That's a good book," Joe said. "I know it well."

Then, unable to contain his curiosity any longer, Joe asked, "Robbie, who was that man who slapped you yesterday? And why did he hit you?"

Robbie grimaced. "That's what I came here for. I wanted to thank you for trying to help me. I am sorry for running away, but I was scared."

"But why—" Joe started to press the point, when Frank interrupted him.

"Hey, I think something's happening!" He was watching Ace's door.

The Hardys stood up and peered out into the hallway. They waited a few moments, then Joe shrugged.

"I saw the knob move." Frank explained. "But I suppose he changed his mind about going out."

When they turned back, Robbie was standing. "I'd better go," the boy declared. "Just thank you."

"No problem at all," Frank said. "But don't you want to tell us what happened?"

Robbie's smile was replaced with tension. "Don't worry about it."

"Who was the man slapping you?" Joe persisted.

"I don't know."

"Robbie, we're trying to help you," Frank said firmly. "Tell us. Who is Scrabby? Who is Meeb? What is it they want you to get for them?"

Robbie rushed to the door. "I have to go!" he insisted nervously. "It's late. My mother worries a lot."

"Who is your mother?" Joe asked.

But Robbie didn't answer. He pushed past them and ran down the hall.

"Well, we couldn't very well hold him and give him the third degree," Frank murmured. "But I'm worried about him. That kid's headed for trouble."

"Maybe he'll confide in us eventually," Joe said. "Let's keep an eye on him."

Frank nodded. "The trouble is, we don't even know who he is! I wish he'd told us his last name or who his mother is."

"Did you notice how he kept his hand in his left pocket all the time?" Joe said. "The whole thing is very strange."

Two hours later, Frank was sleeping, while Joe sat in darkness by the slightly open door. He looked at his watch—two more hours until Frank would take his place.

Suddenly, Ace's door opened. The athlete

slipped out without a sound, making sure the door was locked behind him. He went down the hallway toward the entrance.

Frank was wide awake and on his feet a second after his brother touched him.

"Ace just left his room and is on his way out," Joe said.

"Let's go!" Frank said, pulling on his shoes.

4 Danger In The Dark

They waited until they were sure Ace had left the building, then they dashed down to the front door. Joe peeked through the window. "He's going toward Main Street and moving quickly."

The brothers crept out the entrance and silently ran after the athlete. They stayed about twenty-five yards behind, keeping to the shadows and darting from tree to tree.

They watched Ace cross the street. "He's going into that all-night food store," whispered Joe.

Frank shook his head, chuckling softly. "It

sure would be something if we chased him because he's suddenly hungry."

Ten minutes later, Ace emerged, carrying a large store bag. "It looks like he's going to feed an army," Joe said.

Some distance ahead, a car's parking lights flicked on. As the unsuspecting Ace started across the street the automobile glided forward, moving slowly with a low hum. Suddenly, the headlights flashed on and the vehicle roared ahead at top speed. The startled student stood paralyzed as the car headed straight for him.

The Hardy boys, used to quick action, dashed into the street. As Joe was closer, he reached Ace first. Coming in low, he grabbed the athlete's waist and pushed him back. They both fell into the gutter.

The car went by at such a high speed that Frank was unable to see the rear license number. Moments later the car turned into another street on two tires. They could hear it fading away.

Frank helped both young men to their feet. "Are you two all right?" he asked anxiously.

"I'm okay," Joe said.

Ace brushed off his clothes. "I'm all right, I guess, but I think I was hit by a grizzly bear."

He looked at Joe. "You sure can tackle. If you go to college, come to State, will you?"

Joe accepted this accolade with uncharacteristic shyness. After all, the remark was praise indeed from the football player he admired so much for his skills on the gridiron.

"I suppose that was an accident, too," Frank said.

Ace stopped brushing himself. "It must have been," he said evasively. "Whoever was driving wasn't trying to hurt me or anything."

"Oh, come on. These aren't all coincidences. Admit it, someone is out to get you!"

Ace shrugged his shoulders. "All right, someone is out to get me. But I tell you, I don't know who he is or why!"

"Maybe it's because of the Northern game. You take what that guy Camor said this afternoon—"

Ace cut Frank off. "No, it hasn't anything to do with him. Look, I'm sorry I acted today as I did. And thanks, Joe, for knocking me out of the path of that car. But don't ask me any more questions."

Helped by the Hardys, he picked up the cans and boxes of groceries that he had dropped when the automobile charged him. Then he went on toward the dormitory. After a minute, Frank and Joe continued to trail him.

"He's right in one way," Frank said. "That driver wasn't trying to hit him."

"What do you mean?"

"The guy swerved at the last second."

"Hmm." Joe thought about that for a moment. "Did you get a look at him?"

"I had an impression that he was male, but that's all. Everything was happening so fast that it was like a speeded-up motion picture—a blur. I didn't even see his license plate."

Joe, who had been staring ahead at the striding Ace, put his hand on Frank's arm. "There's another guy trailing our friend!"

"They don't give up, do they? Well, let's get this one."

Once again, they moved stealthily through the dark shadows of the campus trees. They were within a few yards of the person when Joe stubbed his foot against a rock. "Ouch," he said involuntarily.

Startled, the person following Ace heard the exclamation and started to run.

"I'll follow Ace," Frank hissed. "Get that guy!"

For the second time in twenty-four hours, Joe found himself in a chase. This time he was determined to succeed. He soon realized that the stranger was not the same person who had shoved Ace off the library steps. This one was much slower. Joe was about to tackle him, but changed his mind and just grabbed his shoulder. The man stopped immediately and cowered.

Joe spun him around. "Professor Overton!" he exclaimed.

He could see relief in the instructor's face. "Are you Joseph or Frank?"

"Joseph. Joe Hardy. Why were you running away?"

"I . . . I . . . excuse me while I catch my breath." A minute later, Overton continued. "I've been worried about Ace Harrington. I heard the rumors of these mysterious attempts on his life and, of course, they were confirmed when you were appointed to watch him. I thought that I would go by his room to see if everything was all right. I was crossing the campus when I saw Harrington walking from the direction of Main Street. I was just about to call to him when I saw he was being followed."

"Yes, by us," Joe said in exasperation.

"No, not by you. By someone else."

Joe was incredulous. "Ace must be the most watched guy in the world, outside of the president."

"Well, then I heard someone behind me. Without thinking, I ran. I fear I'm not the most courageous person in the world."

"We'd better check on this new guy fast," Joe said. "Come on, Professor."

Meanwhile, Frank saw Ace enter the dormitory. He ran up to the front door and saw the football player enter his room. Relieved, Frank went down the steps again to wait for Joe.

Suddenly, four men emerged from the shadows of the building behind him. Before Frank even knew they were there, his arms were pinioned by two of them. He struggled, but it was no use. The other two walked around to face him.

"I thought you guys got the word," one of the strangers said. "Harry said to lay off."

"Harry who?"

"Don't get smart with me," the man snarled. "We know who you are and you know who we are. We told you once: don't hurt the Harrington kid!"

"We're not trying to hurt him," Frank said.

"Don't give me that," the other man sneered. "We saw you just now trying to shove Ace in front of a car."

"You've got it all wrong!" Frank protested. "We pushed him *out* of the way."

"That's the way it looked to me," the other

man in front confirmed.

"Shut up!" the leader snapped. "I know what I saw."

"You're crazy!" Frank protested. "We—"

"Shut up." The man swung his fist and slammed Frank on the side of the head. The boy kicked forward. His shoe smashed against his attacker's knee. The man slumped to the ground, clutching his leg. "Give it to him, Hank!"

The other man in front stepped forward and delivered a tremendous blow to Frank's stomach. The young detective thought he was going to pass out. His vision was a blur and he gasped for breath.

Just then Joe and Professor Overton came around the corner of the building. "What's going on?" Joe demanded.

"Stay away, kid," the leader growled as he rose to his feet, "or you'll get what your pal got."

Joe doubled his fists and started forward. Frank recovered enough to say, "Stay there . . . Joe. I think . . . they're almost . . . finished."

"That's right," said the leader. "We're going. Tell Camor to lay off Harrington if he knows what's good for him. This is the second warning and it's the last. Next time, Harry will come, too, and Camor knows what that will mean."

"We're not Camor's—" Joe said, but was cut off by Frank.

"Who's Harry?" asked Frank.

"Don't give me that! You know who we're talking about. Harry Weller, of course." The leader gave a signal to his men. They released Frank and disappeared into the darkness.

Joe and Professor Overton helped Frank to the dormitory steps where he sat down to recover his breath. "That . . . guy has some . . . punch," Frank said. "How come . . . you're here, Professor?"

Joe quickly explained how he had caught up to the professor and the reason Overton was stalking Ace.

"We appreciate it," Frank said, "but it's not necessary. In fact, it kind of . . . hampers our work. It takes all our effort to guard Ace without any complications."

"I understand fully," the teacher said gravely. "I'm only in the way." He glanced in the direction the thugs had gone. "Especially when a bunch of hoodlums mistake you for somebody else. Well, I'll say good night now. Keep up the good work."

Frank was able to rise comfortably by this time. As they were walking down the dormitory hall, they heard talking from Ace's room. The boys looked at each other with curiosity.

Frank knocked at the athlete's door. "Are you okay, Ace?"

The talking stopped immediately. In a moment, Ace opened the door enough for him to slip out and close the door behind him.

"Sure, I'm fine." He studied Frank. "But you don't look too good. You seem out of breath. You ought to exercise more, get in shape."

"He *is* out of breath," Joe said. "It was knocked out of him." He described what had happened at the dormitory steps.

Ace's face was a picture of confusion. "Harry Weller? I never heard of him. Camor, yes, I know him, not that I want to. Weller, definitely not."

Then he grinned. "So Professor Overton was trailing me because he was worried. He's a real oddball, and he's so obsessed by this project of his. You know, he's let me work on a small part of it, which is an honor. In fact, the project is all he thinks of night or day so it's really unbelievable that he took the trouble to trail me."

"Ace, we heard talking in your room," Frank said.

The athlete's face turned to stone. "It's just the radio," he said. "Good night. See you tomorrow." With that, he disappeared behind the door.

The boys went to their room. "Do you notice that when Ace wants to avoid talking about something, he says good-bye and walks away?" Joe asked.

Frank chuckled. "I guess it's better than getting into an argument."

Joe switched on the overhead light. "Look!"

Frank followed his brother's pointing finger. On the opposite wall was a paper pinned by a wicked-looking knife. The boys could read the printing from a distance: MIND YOUR OWN BUSINESS!

Frank walked across and pulled out the knife. He reread the warning. "Written in crayon. But by whom? These new guys—the Harry Weller group—caught up to us outside, so why would they bother warning us again? Also, from the way the leader talked, they really didn't know much about us. It's much more likely to be Camor's gang."

"How do you think they got in?" Joe wondered. "The door was locked."

"Well, you can't call this lock exactly burglarproof," Frank muttered, inspecting the mechanism. "However, it doesn't look as if it was jimmied."

Joe snapped his fingers. "The window wasn't open when we left."

43

"That's it!" his brother agreed. "See the table in front of the window? It's all messed up. The pen-and-pencil set has been knocked over, three books are on the floor, and a water glass is broken."

Joe nodded glumly. "There's another possibility—the big guy who tried to push Ace down the library steps could have come in here."

"Or Scrabby," Frank said.

Joe shook his head. "That's a long shot. How does he know who we are?"

Before Frank could reply, loud footsteps in the hall caused them to spin around and face the still open door. Robbie came charging in, looking as if a ghost were chasing him. "Scrabby's after me! He almost caught me!"

"Calm down, you're safe now," Joe commanded. "We'll head him off."

Frank and Joe left the frightened youth pacing the room. There was no one in the hall, but they heard the click of the front door closing. The Hardys ran to it and looked out of the adjacent window, seeing the back of a huge man lumbering into the darkness.

In a flash, they were out of the door and took up pursuit. However, the man had disappeared between the trees and was nowhere to be seen.

Discouraged, they returned to their room. Robbie was gone!

"The window!" Joe cried.

They stared out just in time to see the boy vanishing around a corner of the building.

"You stay here," Joe said to his brother. "I'll go after him!" He climbed out the window, jumped to the ground, and ran after the fleeing boy.

5 No Comment

Joe returned in a few minutes. "No luck. That kid is tricky. I almost had my hands on him when he suddenly jumped. So I fell over a small chain fence used to keep people off the grass. I almost broke my leg. When I got up, he was gone."

He examined his torn jeans. "Frank, do you think I'm losing my speed? I've chased three people in the last twenty-four hours. I lost two of them and the only one I caught was a middle-aged, out-of-shape professor."

"Of course, you're losing your speed, little brother," Frank said in a kidding tone. "It's becoming very noticeable. You're growing old rapidly. By next week, you ought to be hobbling along on a cane."

Joe threw a pillow at Frank, who laughed and ducked. "I think it's my turn to watch," Frank said, "while you get some shuteye."

"No. You took quite a punch out there," Joe said. "You rest. I'll wake you in an hour." Frank protested, but Joe held up his hand pompously with a mischievous sparkle in his eye. "Remember, I won't be a very old man until next week."

At six in the morning, the three young men jogged again. Frank ran easily and appeared to have recovered from the punch he had received.

Once more the Hardys accompanied the sports star to his classes and lectures. Everywhere they went, the campus hero was looked at with envy and admiration. He had a good word for everyone, but both Frank and Joe had the feeling that Ace was uncomfortable with all the adulation.

As they were eating lunch in the student center, a stocky young man approached, carrying his tray from the food line. "Do you mind if I sit?" he asked Ace.

"Help yourself," Ace said. "Joe and Frank, meet Tank Ritter, tackle supreme and my oldest friend here at State."

The boys' hands almost disappeared in Tank's huge fists during a vigorous handshake. "Glad to meet you," he said as he gnawed on a hamburger. "What Ace said is right. We came to State on the same bus." He chuckled. "I hate to admit it, but we were kind of scared."

Ace laughed. "And green! We wandered around most of the day, trying to find our dorms. We didn't ask anyone because we didn't want to look dumb."

"We were that way for three weeks." Tank's face lit up at the remembrance. Then he became sober. "Ace, I wish you'd come over and stay with me for a while."

"Why?"

"Don't kid your old pal. I know what everyone else knows. Someone's after you. Being on the ground floor makes you a sitting pigeon. I live on the fourth floor. They'll have a hard time getting at you up there."

Ace smiled. "Sure. Then they would have to take the elevator. Look, Tank, I appreciate your concern, but I'm doing okay where I am. Anyhow, I have two bodyguards." He pointed at Frank and Joe.

48

Tank looked at the Hardys critically. "I know you have a fine reputation and all that, but guarding Ace is a real tough job. Do you think you're up to it?"

"What he means," Ace said in a mocking tone, "is why aren't you built like him. Tank, thanks a lot. I've got to run to an early physics lab this afternoon."

Professor Overton was not as outgoing as he had been at the laboratory the day before. He smiled briefly at the boys and said hello, but spent most of the two hours walking around and checking papers at his desk.

Frank commented about this on their way downstairs to football practice.

"He does get moody at times," Ace admitted, "and today he's worse than I've ever seen him. He wouldn't talk to me about the formula I handed in yesterday—he said he was too busy." Ace shook his head in pity. "What a solitary life he has. He lives all alone in an apartment on campus and does nothing but work."

The stadium was sprinkled with reporters. They tried to swarm around the team, but Coach Bradley chased them back into the stands. "You can talk to anyone you want to after practice, but right now we have some serious business to do."

It was only a light scrimmage, but the reporters scribbled or talked into tape recorders as if it had been a big game. After Ace took a punt on his twenty-yard line and snaked down through an entire junior varsity team, the news people applauded.

When it was over, the reporters ran onto the field again. Coach Bradley lifted his arms. "Hold it. I know that all of you are anxious to interview Ace, so suppose he stays out here for"—he looked at his wristwatch—"fifteen minutes. And I do mean fifteen minutes, not a second more." He turned to the rest of the players. "You guys go inside. You all looked pretty sloppy today. If you play like that on Saturday, Northern will mop up the field with you. I've got to go over some fundamentals with you that you obviously have forgotten."

"Frank, I'd like to go along," Joe whispered. "Maybe I can pick up some pointers because all of them looked pretty good to me."

"Okay," Frank said. "I'll hold the fort out here."

Joe followed the team inside and then took a seat in the back of the locker room. Coach Bradley stood in front.

"I've heard you all grumbling, saying you think you did well today, that you don't deserve this talk." He paused for dramatic effect and

50

then grinned. "And you're right! You looked sharp. Now don't let this rare praise on my part go to your heads. It's one thing to be all-Americans on a weekday, but what happens after the kickoff Saturday is what counts.

"I went through that act out on the field because I wanted to talk to you alone—without Ace, I mean—and I didn't want any of those newsmen around.

"Ace has almost been badly injured several times in the past two weeks. You no doubt know part of the story, but not all of it." He enumerated the various attacks in detail.

"We've heard about some of the attacks," one of the players admitted.

The coach nodded. "We're doing everything we can to protect Ace. The administration has hired the famous Hardy boys to guard him, for example. You can help, too, by keeping an eye out for any suspicious characters. Report any of them to me. Yes, Fred?"

A tall player whom Joe recognized as Fred Lee, all-conference tight end, had risen and was whispering to Coach Bradley. He nodded toward Joe.

"No, that's Joe Hardy," Bradley told him, "But thanks for your alertness. Now to continue."

Frank was bored. He thought news conferences were exciting, but the sports reporters were asking what he felt were silly questions.

"Are you nervous about next week's game?"

"How does it feel to be an all-American?"

"What's the game plan for Northern?"

Then came the bombshell in the form of a query from a West Coast writer. "I hear that you have been seen recently with a well-known gambler. What do you say to that?"

Ace flushed. "Who told you that?"

The reporter calmly met the athlete's gaze. "You know news sources are confidential. Would you please answer my question, Mr. Harrington?"

"No comment!"

Suddenly, Ace was bombarded with questions related to gambling. The star repeated again and again, "No comment." At last, he strode out, almost running to the locker room with the reporters chasing him to the door.

Frank followed at a discreet distance. He skirted the writers who were either chatting in small knots or looking for pay phones. He entered the locker room to find Ace had gone to the shower. Coach Bradley was still talking to the team.

Tank Ritter jumped up. "If anyone tries to hurt Ace, I'm going to bust him up!"

"That's the right attitude, Tank, but not the right action. Turn the culprit over to the police."

"I sure will, coach," the tackle said, "*after* I bust him up!"

The team laughed, and even Coach Bradley smiled. "I guess that's the right note to end on." He walked over to Joe and Frank, holding out his hand. "Ace pointed you out to me yesterday. The best of luck to both of you. If I can help you in any way, please let me know. How did it go in the news conference? Ace handles himself well with reporters."

Frank quickly summed up what had occurred. The coach turned pale. "Gamblers? Is any of it true?"

The Hardys looked at each other. "Well, I'm afraid that a gambler called Sureshot Camor has been bothering him," Frank said.

The coach's hands doubled into fists. "I know that little rat. Sureshot is the right name. He'll do anything to make sure his bets will win. Ace should have told me about it. I'll talk to him—"

"With all due respect, Mr. Bradley, I wouldn't right now. He's in no mood for it," Frank said.

Bradley nodded. "I was wondering why he slammed in here and went straight in to his shower without saying a word to anyone. I'll lay off for today. But I'll have to talk to him tomorrow."

He went into his office. A moment later, Ace joined the Hardys. "Let's go," he said. His face showed that he would not tolerate any questions.

He led them through a back entrance to the locker room and they emerged outside the stadium. He had just breathed a sigh of relief when they were surrounded by a mass of chanting students. Many of them held signs: DOWN WITH PROFESSIONAL COLLEGE SPORTS and NO MORE ATHLETIC SCHOLARSHIPS.

Ace started to push his way through the crowd. In doing so, he inadvertenly shoved a couple of students, who fell to the ground.

"Harrington, use words, not muscles. You don't have to show how much of an athlete you are out here!" The speaker was a pretty dark-haired young woman who stepped in front of the football player.

"Who are you?" Ace demanded.

"Carol Crider, president of Students Against Professional Athletes, better known as SAPA!"

"Oh, yes, I've read your articles in the college newspaper. But why pick on me? Picket the administration."

"Oh, we've done that. Reporters can see us

down here. We're not picking on you. It's athletic scholarships we're against."

"What's wrong with them? I have one and I've been keeping up with my studies without taking any easy courses!"

She wasn't going to be put off by such logic. "Giving scholarships for playing games is wrong," she insisted. "It keeps out deserving students."

"In case you don't know, I would not have been able to come here if I didn't have a scholarship. But I also wouldn't be allowed to play if I didn't prove myself academically."

Just then Coach Bradley and the team emerged from the stadium. Tank Ritter advanced ominously toward the crowd with his fists up. "I'm going to bust a few of your heads for bothering Ace!"

The coach pushed him back. "Calm down," he ordered.

"Look, they're just talking to me," Ace added. "Don't worry about it."

"I think it's about time you started worrying about what people think!" Carol cried out. "Anyway, this isn't the last you've heard of us!" She stamped her foot and walked away.

6 Kidnapped!

Ace shrugged and left, followed by the Hardys.

When they reached the dorm, he said, "You know, I don't feel like having supper tonight. Also, I've got some heavy studying to do."

"Sure, Ace," Joe said. "We understand."

Frank went to town, bought take-out food, and carried it back to the room. "This is good for a change," Joe said. "There's not so much noise or crowding." He bit into his roast beef sandwich.

"One day away from home and I miss Aunt Gertrude's food," Frank said.

They watched TV until eleven. Joe was about to get ready for bed when Ace poked his head into the room.

"I'm going downtown to get some chow. I guess you want to come along."

"We sure do," Frank said.

They accompanied him to the same grocery store he had gone to the night before.

"You mostly buy cans," Joe observed as Ace filled a bag. "How come?"

"It's easier for me," Ace said. "I get hungry at odd times. I have a hotplate but no refrigerator."

When they entered the dormitory again, they were met by an excited group of students. One of them said, "Hey, Ace, some guys broke into your room and—"

Ace dropped his bag and ran through the open door. A scene of confusion was inside. A table and two chairs had been knocked over.

"Bill's been kidnapped!" Ace yelled.

"Who is Bill?" Frank asked.

"My brother!"

Ace dashed out of the room and ran down the hall. Frank and Joe followed, but by the time they reached the outside, Ace had disappeared! Frank thought quickly. Where could the kidnappers have taken Ace's brother? And where could Ace have gone?

"To the parking lot!" Frank shouted.

When the Hardys arrived at the entrance, the yellow lights revealed Ace struggling with four men next to a car. He had knocked one of them down and was hitting another, but a third thug slipped up behind the athlete and slugged him with a blackjack. Ace slumped, and his assailant pushed him through the open back door. The four kidnappers then jumped into the automobile and sped off just before Frank and Joe reached them.

Joe slammed his fist into the open palm of his other hand in frustration, while Frank took a small notebook and wrote down the license plate number. Then they ran to a phone booth at the edge of the lot and phoned police headquarters. After identifying himself, Frank was connected with Chief Higgins at the official's home. Frank summed up the situation succinctly, relating only the important details.

"Frank Hardy, eh?" said Chief Higgins. "I've met your father a few times and I think he's the best cop I've ever been acquainted with. Have you got a CB?"

"In our car, yes."

"Okay. Put on channel eleven. That's the police channel. We'll keep you informed. Right now I'm going to get my staff in operation."

Frank and Joe sat in the car with their CB radio on. "What do we do now?" Joe asked.

Before Frank could answer, the CB crackled. "That car was rented in New York City to Albert Camor," the chief reported. "I have issued a three-state alarm. Roadblocks have been set up on every major artery in the state and on every road leading out of town."

"Thanks, Chief Higgins."

"What are you fellows going to do?"

"We're not quite sure yet," Frank replied.

"Well, if you run across something, let me know," Higgins said.

"You can count on that!" Frank said and cut off. "Joe, what would you do if you were Camor?"

"I wouldn't try to get out of town. Since the Hardys saw me and probably have figured out who I was and informed the police, I'd hide somewhere around here."

"Where? You could go to relatives, but it's improbable that you have any here."

"A hotel?" Joe suggested.

"Hotels have lobbies. Imagine taking the prisoners—perhaps unconscious—through a lobby. It'd be pretty difficult to pass through unnoticed."

"Boat?"

"That would be fine in Bayport, but there's only a very shallow river passing by here and no pleasure craft."

Joe snapped his fingers. "A motel where you

don't have to go through a lobby, where you could drive right up to your door and hardly anyone would notice what you took out of your car."

"So we look for motels." Frank contacted Chief Higgins on the CB again and informed him of their plan.

"That will be a big help," the police officer said. "To be truthful, I just don't have the staff to handle roadblocks and patrol the city streets, too. As a matter of fact, I've already asked the state police to lend a hand and they're sending over a few people."

"We'll be glad to do anything we can," Frank assured him.

"Thanks. Now I wish I had good news for you, but I don't," Chief Higgins continued. "I phoned Dr. Catello. I always call him in a serious matter that concerns the university. He was pretty angry and put the blame on you guys, which I don't think is fair. Anyway, he said something like, 'I thought they were too young.' I'm afraid you two are in his doghouse."

"I can't blame him," Frank said. "After all, we were hired to watch over Ace. Well let's hope we find him."

"Good luck!" Higgins signed off.

The boys stopped at an all-night drugstore

and checked the yellow pages of the city's phone book. There were six motels—three in the north end and three in the southern part of the metropolis near the university.

Since they were in the southern area, they started their search there. The first motel was a single two-story building with few separate entrances. The two youths questioned the desk clerk, but discovered that no one answering the rogues' descriptions had taken a room.

They were driving to the second motel when Frank said, "Look, there's Scrabby!"

The gigantic man was walking down the street, stopping here and there, as if looking for something or someone.

"Let's talk to him," Joe said.

"We haven't time," Frank objected, but then remembered Robbie's terrified face. "All right, but not for long."

He pulled over to the curb and Joe opened his window. "Hey, Mr. Scrabby," he called.

The giant glared at him.

"You'd better stop hounding Robbie or you'll end up in prison."

Scrabby snarled like a wild beast and charged at the car. He was very fast for his size, and Frank pulled away just in time. "I didn't really expect him to listen," he said.

"But at least now he knows Robbie's got friends who'll watch out for him," Joe observed.

They had no luck at the second motel. As soon as they got in the car again, there was a message from the chief over the CB. "I thought you would like to know that the kidnappers' car was found on Second Street, about three blocks from where you are. A superficial examination didn't give us the shadow of a clue. But the auto is in our garage right now and our experts are going over it inch by inch."

"Thanks, Chief," Frank said. "You narrowed our search."

"What did you mean by that?" Joe asked when Frank switched off the CB. "How did he narrow our search?"

"I figured that the kidnappers wouldn't dump the car near their motel. They would drive it to another part of the city. So their motel probably is—"

"In the north end of town," Joe concluded.

At the first two motels, they found nothing, and Frank was beginning to doubt his theory. But at the third, they hit their mark.

The desk clerk at the Moonrise Motel was reluctant to talk to them about the establishment's guests. "After all, how do I know you are who you say you are? You show me cards with your names, but that's really no proof."

They showed him their driver's licenses, but the man said, "You could have forged those."

At last, the Hardys became exasperated and called police headquarters. They asked for Chief Higgins and then handed the phone to the clerk. His face showed relief as he hung up. "The chief vouches for you. I have a very tough boss and he'd fire me if I allowed anything to happen that wasn't on the level."

"We understand," Joe said.

"I don't know of any Camor registered in this motel, but I have an odd group living in room twenty-nine at the end of row C. Your description of Sureshot fits the guy they call boss. He was the one who signed the register. Here's his signature!"

The name was William Romac. The boys looked at each other, hearts pounding. They were sure they had caught the right man. They both saw immediately that "Romac" was "Camor" spelled backwards!

"All you have to do is go down to the first row and turn left," the cooperative clerk said.

Frank nodded. "Thanks!"

He and Joe were walking toward row C when they suddenly heard the sounds of a struggle and yelling from that direction!

7 The Eavesdropper

A few moments later, a car shot out from between the buildings, almost knocking them over. There obviously was a struggle going on in the back seat. Frank and Joe could see two shadowy figures pushing each other down. The automobile's lights were out and the boys were unable to see the license plate.

Fearing that time was running out, they hurried to the end of row C where the desk clerk had said Romac's room was. The door was slightly open, but there was no sound coming from inside.

"Oh-oh," Joe said, preparing for the worst.

They pushed the door open but stood several

steps away. There was a groan and they could see a man lying on the floor, tightly bound.

Frank and Joe entered cautiously, but one glance showed them they were in no danger. Besides the man on the floor, the only other inhabitant in the room was a youth lying on the bed. He was tied and gagged. He looked at them with terrified eyes.

"You know who I think that is?" Joe asked.

Frank nodded. "Ace's brother. And the guy on the floor is Sureshot Camor. Let's untie Bill first."

They were loosening the boy's bonds when the desk clerk stuck his head in. "I heard some noise and I thought I would investi—" He looked around at the wreckage. "What on earth happened?"

"A fight," Joe said.

"Why did you fight with—"

"Not us," Frank snapped. "We hardly had time for that, did we? You can do us a big favor. Phone the police, ask for Chief Higgins, and tell him that the Hardys are at the Moonrise Motel, that we have Camor, but Ace is nowhere in sight."

"Sure!" The clerk dashed away.

"You're with the police?" the boy asked as the gag was removed.

"Kind of," Joe said. "You're Ace's brother, Bill?"

Alarm showed in the boy's eyes. "Why do you think so?"

"Are you?"

"Ace said it was supposed to be a secret and if anyone saw me, I wasn't to admit it."

"We weren't aware you were living in his room," Frank said, "but he blurted out your name when he was chasing after the kidnappers. He also mentioned that you were his brother."

"If you're the Hardys," the boy went on, "you're the guys who were supposed to guard him."

"And a fine job we did of it," Joe said bitterly.

"Come on, Joe, it's not our fault and you know it," Frank said. "Ace wouldn't wait for us. Now, Bill, tell us all that happened."

"Ace told me you were a couple of honest guys," Bill said, "so I'll trust you. I was in a foster home in Chicago. It—it was just terrible, so I ran away. I hitchhiked here. Ace said if the police found me, I'd be sent back, so he's been hiding me in his room for a couple of weeks. He was trying to see if I could stay with a friend's family, but they're away on vacation."

"That's why he's been going out at night to get you food!" Frank declared. "Now it all makes sense." Then he turned to Sureshot, who was staring at them with hatred. "How'd *you* get into this?" he demanded.

Bill answered for the gambler. "Somehow this guy and his gang found out that I was living in Ace's room. He said he would tell the police I was there unless Ace played so badly on Saturday that Northern would win. But Ace refused. I also heard that guy on the floor—"

"Sureshot," Joe informed him.

"Yeah, Sureshot, say his men tried to injure Ace, but it didn't work. Wow, my wrists and ankles are numb from those ropes." Bill sat on the edge of the bed and rubbed his arms.

Sureshot kicked his feet on the floor to get attention.

"Take it easy," Frank told him and turned back to Bill. "What happened tonight?"

"I was waiting for Ace to come back with the food when a bunch of men smashed down the door and came into the room. I tried to get past them, but they blocked my way. I pushed some chairs and a table at them, but they shoved them to one side. They grabbed me and hauled me out to a car.

"They were just about to drive away when Ace came. They hit him with something and yanked him into the car."

"We saw that," Joe put in.

Bill nodded. "Then they brought us here and tied us up."

"After that what happened?" Frank asked.

"This guy on the floor, Sureshot, he was waiting. He was mad as anything that they had brought Ace. He said nobody would care much that I was kidnapped and anyhow Ace would never tell anyone since he didn't want me to go back to the foster home in Chicago. But, he said, they'll send out the army, navy, and marines to find Ace. They couldn't get out of town, he said, because the place would be crawling with cops."

"They were right!" Joe said grimly.

"Well, he calmed down at last. He told his men to get rid of the car because it might have been seen going out of the parking lot at the college. He also asked them to pick up some food. I don't know what happened to them. They left over an hour ago."

Joe and Frank laughed. "I don't think that they'll ever come back," Joe said. "No doubt they realized just how bad the situation was. Good work, Sureshot!"

The bound gambler looked disgusted.

"If you fellows had been able to get here a little sooner, you might have rescued Ace," Bill said sadly.

Frank nodded. "We heard some noise that sounded like fighting, and we saw a car pulling away, but that's all we know."

"It happened so fast," Bill said. "There was a knock at the door. Sureshot thought his men were coming back and he was already yelling at them when he opened the door. A bunch of guys I never saw before came in. They hit Sureshot and tied him up. Then they untied Ace, and one of them told him they were going to take him some place where he would be safe. I could see Ace was suspicious. He said he didn't want to go, that he wanted to call the cops. He started for the phone and they grabbed him.

"That was the noise we heard," Joe put in.

Bill nodded. "Ace put up a good fight, but it wasn't any use. There were at least four or five men, and it took all of them to drag him out of the door. Then you came and I thought you were some of that gang returning."

Sirens blasted the air, and they could hear the squeal of brakes. In a moment, police led by Chief Higgins poured into the room. He looked at Sureshot. "Who's this?"

Frank explained what had happened as briefly and as completely as he could. Chief Higgins nodded to his men. "Untie him."

69

When the gag was off, Sureshot spluttered, "I've been kept here against my will! I have been assaulted by men who broke in. And I want you to arrest these two—" he pointed to Frank and Joe"—"who chatted with the boy while watching me suffer on the floor."

"Oh, stow it, Camor," the chief said wearily. "You've kept me up most of the night and now you're giving me a headache." His voice turned formal. "You are under arrest. You have the right to remain silent. Anything you say may be held against you in a court of law. If you want an attorney, we will—"

"What!" Sureshot shouted. "I am under arrest? Have you lost your mind? I'm the victim of a crime and the gangsters are getting away. I demand that you immediately send out an alarm for their apprehension."

Chief Higgins went on reciting Camor's rights as if the gambler had never spoken. When he had finished, he added, "Why don't you talk now? Why did you kidnap Ace? Where is he? You know what we want to know, so open up."

"I'm not saying a word until I talk to my lawyer," the gambler stated haughtily.

Higgins shrugged. "If you want to. But I'll tell you, you'll do yourself a world of good if you help us. Figure it out. You are going to be charged with breaking and entering, assault and battery, and—worst of all—kidnapping. If you cooperated now, the judge would take that into consideration."

Sureshot thought for a moment and then said in a sullen tone, "What do you want to know?"

"Who were the guys who came into this room and took away Ace a little while ago?"

"Harry Weller's men."

"And who is Harry Weller?"

Sureshot looked up in surprise. "You don't know? Why, he's one of the biggest gamblers in New York."

"Why did he want Ace when you already had him?"

Camor lifted his hands, palms out in a gesture of ignorance. "How should I know? He sent word to me that I was to lay off Ace, but I don't know any more than that."

"Okay, that's all for now," the chief said to his men. "Take him downtown and book him."

Just then, another police officer came into the room, pushing a husky young man before him. "I don't know if this means anything, Chief, but I found this guy around the back, listening to everything that was said."

The new arrival was Tank Ritter!

71

8 Dismissed

"Who are you," Chief Higgins asked, "and what are you doing here?"

"He's Tank Ritter," Frank explained when the student remained quiet and confused, "a tackle on the university's football team. Supposedly, Ace is his best friend on the campus."

"Yeah, that's it," Tank said hurriedly. "I'm his best friend. I heard something about him being kidnapped and I came here looking for him."

Everybody in the room was silent as they stared at the young man.

"That's very nice of you," Higgins said, smiling. "I like loyalty to friends."

Tank beamed.

The police official continued, "One or two things bother me, though, son. Maybe you can help clear them up."

Tank nodded vigorously. "I'd be glad to do anything, sir."

The smile disappeared and Chief Higgins's voice sharpened. "How did you know Ace was kidnapped?"

"Why . . . why, I heard it on the radio."

"You must have some radio since we kept this whole affair under wraps. No newspaper, no TV reporter, no radio station has been notified. Also, how did you happen to come to help your good old friend Ace at this particular motel? The Hardys only found out it was Camor's hideout within the last hour. Did you hear that over the radio, too?"

Tank hung his head. "I'm ashamed of myself, sir. I was trying to appear a hero. You're right. I didn't know Ace had been kidnapped and brought here. I came over to reserve a room for the weekend for my grandmother, who is coming to see the Northern game. When I got here, I saw the police cars so I sneaked around to see what was up. I heard what was being said so I decided, when the officer nabbed me, to act as if I knew what was going on all the time."

Higgins shook his head. "I'll give you one thing, Mr. Ritter, you sure know how to think fast. You dream up lies quickly—not well, but quickly. You don't really expect me to believe that malarkey about your grandmother, do you?"

"It's the truth!" Tank exclaimed.

"If I called in the desk clerk, would he confirm that story?"

"I never got that far," Tank cried desperately. "I saw the police cars and—"

"Stop your sniveling, Tank," Sureshot Camor snarled. "I'll tell you, Chief, why he was here and remember that I'm doing this in a spirit of cooperation."

"I shall put in my report that you were most eager to do your duty as a citizen."

Sureshot ignored the sarcasm. "He was here to get money from me!"

"And why would you pay him?"

"Shut up, Sureshot, shut up!" Tank yelled desperately.

The gambler looked at him with contempt. "You jumped at the chance when I offered it to you. You're in it as deeply as I am."

Higgins closed his eyes. "Let's stop all this bickering. Mr. Camor, I repeat my question. Why did you pay him?"

"He was to cause accidents to happen to Ace. He didn't do a very good job of it, though."

"Is that true, Mr. Ritter?"

The football player kept his eyes glued to the floor.

"I take silence to mean assent, but you can take all that up with your lawyer later on. In the meantime, I'm booking you." Once again, Chief Higgins recited an arrested person's rights. "Okay, men, take them both away."

After Sureshot and Tank had left the room, Higgins turned to the Hardys. "I certainly appreciate your work. I can see your father has trained you well. Congratulations. What are you going to do now?"

"We'll get Bill back to college so he can go to bed . . . unless you want him for something," Frank said.

"Not me. I don't have any warrants from Illinois demanding his return. I'm keeping hands off. I figure that Ace and the university can come up with some solution between them. If I were you, though, I would go see President Catello right now. He told me he would stay up until he received some news."

"He won't be happy," Joe said ruefully.

"He's apt to be a little tense, I admit," said the chief. "Do you want me to phone him and tell him about the fine work you have done so far?"

Frank shook his head. "Thank you for the offer, but I think we'd better face the music alone."

"Okay, then, I'll be going. You know, the roadblocks are still up and will stay up until we catch Weller's gang. It's nearly impossible to get out of the city."

On the way back to the university, Bill became talkative. "I sure hope they find Ace pretty fast. He's the best guy in the world. I'm not saying that because he's my brother, either. I've known some kids whose brothers are terrible. But Ace has always tried to take care of me."

"Why did you run away from the foster home?" Joe asked.

"Since my mother died, I've been in a lot of foster homes. Most of them have been pretty good. But the people who ran this last one just wanted the money. They're not nice to any of the kids there. They didn't give us enough food, and we were always being punished for little things. They didn't even let me go see my father in the hospital."

"That's really rough," Frank sympathized.

"Well, I finally couldn't take it any more. I took off one night and hitchhiked to State. Ace put me up."

"Didn't any of the people who picked you up on the road wonder why a kid like you was on the road?"

Bill shrugged. "I'd always have some kind of story for them. None of them seemed to bother to check up. There are a lot of kids hitching nowadays."

"And Ace was planning to place you with friends of his?" Frank asked.

"Right. His friend John told him his parents would probably take me, but he couldn't ask them because they're away on a trip for a month."

The downstairs lights were on in the beautiful house of President Catello at the edge of the campus. The Hardys and Bill got out of the car and walked up the steps to the wide porch. Before they could ring the doorbell, the door opened and the scowling president stood there in a bathrobe.

"Come in," he said in an angry tone of voice.

Leading them to his panelled study, he waved them to seats while he remained standing.

"Police Chief Higgins phoned me a few minutes ago and informed me you were on the way. I suppose I should be glad that Ace's *first* kidnappers have been found—apparently by you—and that Mr. Ritter has been exposed as the perpetrator of those attempts to hurt Harrington.

"But I am most disturbed that Ace should have been abducted under your very noses in the first place. Now a *second* group of kidnappers has appeared on the scene and Harrington has been whisked away again."

Frank opened his mouth to speak, but the college president raised his hand. "Who is this?" he said in a softer tone, nodding toward Bill.

Frank explained that Bill was Ace's younger brother and had come from Illinois to get away from his difficult foster family. Catello smiled at the boy. "So you are part of the mystery which has been cleared up. Don't worry. You shall stay here tonight and we'll look for a proper foster home for you near here."

Seeing the boy's elation, Catello patted him on the shoulder, then turned back to the Hardys. "I was concerned about your youth and your ability to handle such an important assignment, but your father dispelled my doubts. However, it would seem that my initial fears were correct."

Frank was annoyed. "If I may be allowed to say so, sir, you seem to lay a great deal of blame on our age. Mozart had written many symphonies at our age, Alexander had conquered a large part of the world, Fernando Valenzuela was a star pitcher . . ."

"But you failed to protect Kevin Harrington," President Catello concluded. "I am afraid that I must discharge you from your duties."

"I guess we have to accept that decision," Frank said with frustration. "Of course, on our own we'll still try to find Ace and return him to the campus."

"That's up to you," the administrator concluded stiffly.

The boys said good-bye to Bill, who wished them luck.

"I sure felt uncomfortable in there," Joe said as they drove to the campus parking lot.

Frank sighed. "You can't win them all."

They parked and walked back across the campus toward the dormitory. "I'm going to miss this place," Joe said. "It was fun being a freshman for a while."

Pops Walzak and one of his men were tidying Ace's room. Frank and Joe stopped and brought him up to date on the night's happenings.

"I'm sorry you got fired," Pops said, "but I'm glad Tank got caught. Imagine knocking your best friend down the library steps!"

"And almost running him over with a car," Joe said. "Of course he only intended to scare Ace."

"It's funny what people will do for money," Pops said. "Oh, say, one of the students took a call on the dormitory hall phone for you. He shoved a note under your door."

"I wonder what that's about," Joe said as he put the key in the lock. "Maybe it was mom."

The note was in big unmistakable letters: ROBBIE STEVENSON IS IN THE HOSPITAL. A DOCTOR PHONED AND SAID YOU SHOULD COME AS SOON AS POSSIBLE. IT IS URGENT!

9 The Gold Bug

They went immediately to the hospital. A nurse at the reception desk told them that Robbie could only be visited by a relative. But when Frank told her their names, she said, "Go right up to room 388. Doctor MacArthur said that Stevenson will not calm down until he talks to you. He's been beaten pretty badly so anything you can do to soothe him will be appreciated."

The boy was tossing and turning and muttering when they entered. His face was a mass of bruises. Frank shook him gently. "Robbie, Frank and Joe Hardy are here."

He looked at them with blurry eyes. "I'm . . . I'm sorry I . . . ran away. I got . . . scared."

"That's all right. Who beat you up?"

Robbie mumbled something that they couldn't hear. Frank leaned down. "What did you say, Robbie?"

The youth's voice rose almost to a scream. "Gold bug!"

"Gold bug? A gold bug beat you up?"

"No, no." Robbie's voice lowered again and his eyes were closing. "Very important, Frank. Gold bug is a—" He stopped talking altogether.

"He's been pretty well sedated," Joe stated.

"If he would only tell us more," Frank said. He leaned down to Robbie's ear and spoke in a normal voice. "What is it about a gold bug? Who beat you up?"

"Why are you hounding my son?" came a commanding voice from the doorway. "Who are you? What are you doing here?"

Frank stood up and faced the newcomer. She was a tall, thin woman with gray hair and a lined face, who was obviously Robbie's mother.

"Didn't you see the 'Do not disturb' sign on the door?" she went on. He needs rest, and lots of it."

"We realize that," Frank said. "We are the—"

"I don't care who you are!" she exclaimed. "Get out of here! For all I know, you may be the very people who beat him up!"

Joe looked at Frank, who shrugged and nodded. They left the room together without attempting another word. "She was very upset," Joe said as they walked down the corridor.

"You can't blame her. Poor kid, getting beaten up like that. It must have been Scrabby."

Joe smiled ruefully. "I certainly didn't manage to scare that creep, did I? You know, this hasn't been one of our great nights."

Frank nodded glumly. "We'd better grab a few hours sleep before we do anything else."

They rested four hours, got up at eight o'clock, and phoned Mr. Hardy in Texas. They told him the woeful news of Ace's kidnapping and their being fired.

"That's too bad," Mr. Hardy said. "You were right, of course, by telling Dr. Catello that you'll keep looking for Ace. He may throw you off the case, but you'll continue working on your own."

"Do you have any good ideas where to start?" Frank asked.

"Get in touch with my friend John Wilensky at the FBI office on River Road," Mr. Hardy advised. "Chief Higgins will report the kidnapping to the FBI and John may have some ideas."

"Thanks, Dad," Frank said.

"But be careful, now. A kidnapping is very tricky, dangerous business."

"We will. You take it easy, too."

Mr. Hardy chuckled. "I hope I'll be home in time for the Northern game. And I'm convinced Ace will be playing."

"I wish I were as confident as dad about that," Frank said after he hung up.

"You're becoming too pessimistic," Joe said. "Let's get going."

On their way to the FBI office, a familiar voice came over the CB. "Bad news, I'm afraid," Police Chief Higgins said. "I've been trying to get hold of you for the last hour to tell you. Weller and his men broke out of the city."

"What?" Frank and Joe cried out together.

"I'm afraid so. It happened just before dawn. His big car crashed a barrier."

"Did your men get the license number?" Joe asked.

"Sure. But a lot of good it did us." The chief's voice was bitter. "We sent out cars in pursuit and had a helicopter hovering above. And guess what? We found the car abandoned two miles away by the side of a road. Tire marks showed a truck was parked there. They just got in the truck and drove away. We haven't the slightest idea what it looks like, but we're going to find out. Believe me."

"So Ace could be almost anywhere now,"

Frank told John Wilensky a few minutes later.

"Well, now that Weller has escaped our trap here," Mr. Wilensky said, "the only place to pick up the trail is in New York City since that's his home territory. I've been in contact with our office there and they'll give us complete cooperation. As a matter of fact, you arrived just in time. I was on my way to the airport, where I have a helicopter waiting. Come on."

Once they were in the air, the boys told the FBI man the entire story of their involvement with Ace, starting with the meeting in Dr. Catello's office.

Wilensky whistled. "It's kind of involved, isn't it, especially with the two rival gangs of gamblers."

When they landed at La Guardia Airport, two agents and a car were waiting. They were whisked away to Weller's office on the top floor of a new skyscraper. Through its wide windows was a view of Manhattan and the Statue of Liberty. The walls were covered with paintings. The boys followed the agents across the thickly carpeted floor.

The three secretaries were closely questioned, but they professed complete ignorance as to the whereabouts of their employer. They had not, they said, seen him in many days.

Undaunted, the agents sped uptown to Harry Weller's apartment. The building superintendent was reluctant to let them in, but when the agents produced a search warrant, he unlocked the door. "I don't know what you can find," he said. "Mr. Weller hasn't been here for a week."

The apartment was even more elaborate than Weller's office. "He certainly lives well," Joe commented.

"For a while, yes," Agent Wilensky said. "Frankly, I've seen many impressive places like this, belonging to gangsters. Eventually all these guys wind up in less pleasant surroundings—in jail, I mean. Crime may pay for a few people, but only for a little while. In the long run, most get caught."

The FBI agents searched the apartment thoroughly, but didn't find a single clue that would tip them off as to where Harry Weller was at the moment.

Discouraged, they were about to leave when Frank accidentally knocked over a heavy ashtray. He was picking it up when he happened to notice a matchbook cover taped to the underside. "Do you think this means anything?" He handed it to John Wilensky. "There are a lot of books and magazines about fishing around the apartment."

The FBI man studied the message on the cover: COME TO CALABOO, NEW HAMPSHIRE, THE BEST INLAND FISHING IN NEW ENGLAND!

"It's a long shot," Wilensky said, "but I would bet on it if I was a betting man. For a guy who loves fishing, Weller sure has a lack of fishing equipment—not a rod or a hook in the house, which means . . ."

". . . he took it with him," Joe ended excitedly.

"Maybe to Calaboo!" Frank concluded.

"Right!" Wilensky was already moving through the door. "Let's go!"

They were listening to music on the radio as they drove toward the airport when the news came on. They were not paying any attention until they heard Ace's name.

". . . switch now to Cliff Moorson, the California sports writer, who made this accusation against Ace Harrington. Cliff, are you there?"

"I sure am, Mike."

"You say that Ace has been bribed to throw the game next Saturday against Northern?"

"I didn't say exactly that. I want to be careful about my statement. I said there is great suspicion concerning Harrington's relationship with a noted gambler. They have been seen together several times. Usually, gamblers do not associate with football players unless they want something. I want to emphasize that I have *not* accused Harrington of taking a bribe."

"What does Ace Harrington say to all this, Cliff?"

"He wouldn't say anything when I questioned him recently. He was evasive, even abusive. I tried to get hold of him today, but apparently he has left the university. I can only speculate that he has disappeared because I exposed him."

"Thank you, Cliff. Word has just come through from the National Collegiate Athletic Association that they have asked State University to bar Ace Harrington from participating in the Northern game unless he can satisfactorily answer the charge brought against him. If State University does not comply with this request, the NCAA will consider that the college is in violation of its rules governing intercollegiate athletics and may be prohibited from all sports for a year.

"We have just received word that our staff has managed to contact Coach Pat Bradley of State by phone," Mike spoke up. "Pat, are you there?"

"I sure am, and broiling, too. That guy Moorson has taken a molehill and made it into a mountain. He has no proof of anything he implied. You will notice that he didn't dare actually say that Ace took a bribe, only that he was talking to a gambler. A football player such as Ace is approached by people all the time and some of them are not what you might call the best of citizens. Is Ace's reputation to be dragged through the mud for this? Listen, I have known this young man for three years and I know he is as honest as the day is long!"

"I'm glad to get your opinion, Coach. But can you tell me where Ace is at the moment and why he hasn't made a public statement concerning this charge?"

"He will answer it in due course. I wish to thank you, Mike, for allowing me this opportunity to defend one of the finest people I have ever known. And I'll see you here on Saturday when we play the game of the century. Goodbye."

"That's it, ladies and gentlemen. You've heard both sides of—"

John Wilensky turned off the radio. He looked grim. "We'd better find this guy fast. Otherwise, he is going to be convicted in the eyes of the public before he has a chance to prove his innocence!"

10 Ace Runs Away

A light passenger plane was waiting for the group at La Guardia Airport. John Wilensky thanked the FBI agents who had been driving them, and a moment later he and the Hardy boys were taking off.

"That Coach Bradley is a shrewd apple." Wilensky chuckled when they were comfortably seated. "He was told by the FBI not to breathe a word that Ace had been kidnapped. Did you notice how he evaded replying when the newscaster asked him where Ace was? Bradley simply said he was ready to defend Harrington, which was obvious. Then he signed off quickly."

"I'm glad he did," Joe said. "I'm sure he's worried about Ace."

The trip took slightly over an hour. They landed in Berlin, New Hampshire, where, once again, three FBI agents met them. Another hour passed before they were driving into Calaboo.

It was a beautiful little community tucked into the mountains which rose on all sides. Through the valley ran a small river with crystal-clear waters.

"Weller? Weller? No, I've never heard of that name in these parts," Mr. Potts, the postmaster and owner of the general store, declared. "And I hear just about everything."

"He probably didn't use his right name," Wilensky said. "Anyway, he was traveling in a large car with a number of men."

A new expression spread over the postmaster's face. "I heard that Caleb Hutchinson rented his cabin to a bunch of fishermen. I never laid sight on 'em myself. Caleb told me about it just before he went over to Boston to visit his daughter. He said they came over to the cabin three days ago, paid the money for one week in advance, and then scooted. Like I said, I never saw them, but I sure heard them. 'Bout five this morning they came through town like speed demons as if they wanted to meet their maker before their time. They made some noise, believe me."

"How do you know they were Caleb Hutchinson's tenants?" Joe asked.

"Because they took the west road and his is the only shack up that way that isn't occupied right now. You take that road, right past the service station. It's about five miles out. Watch you don't miss it. There's a mailbox that has Caleb's name on it, but it's pretty faded. If you don't keep a sharp eye out for it, you might go right past it. The shack is about a quarter mile in from the west road."

The investigators thanked the postmaster and left the store.

"He certainly picked a deserted spot," Wilensky observed. "If you hadn't spotted that matchbook cover, we would have never found him. Of course, we don't know if the people at this cabin are really Weller's gang. We might be on a completely false trail." He looked at the boys. "But I don't think so."

Thanks to Mr. Potts, they found the mailbox. They parked by the side of the road and got out. The four FBI men pulled guns from their pockets.

"You stay here," Wilensky ordered the Hardys. "You might get hurt."

"Mr. Wilensky, Ace is our responsibility.

We'd like to help try to rescue him," Frank pleaded.

The agent looked at their determined faces. "All right," he said at last in a reluctant voice. "But stay at least thirty yards behind. There might be shooting, and your father would have my head if you got hurt."

They promised to obey. The road sloped upward, and cautiously the group climbed, trying to be absolutely silent. The trail went over the top of a ridge and then declined down to the cabin.

On top of the hill, Wilensky signaled for his men to stop and turned to the Hardys. "Take a look down there," he told the Hardys. "Do you see anyone familiar?"

They glanced at a peaceful scene, almost a postcard picture. One man was in the middle of the stream that ran past the cabin, clad in high boots and handling a fishing rod. On the bank sat three others.

"I remember that guy in the middle," Frank said excitedly. "He's the one who punched me!"

"How about you, Joe? You came in at the end of Frank's scuffle with Weller's friends. Do you recognize any?"

"It was pretty dark, Mr. Wilensky," Joe said,

"but I believe I recognize the man Frank pointed out."

"The fisherman is Harry Weller," one of the government agents spoke up. "When I was stationed in Boston, I had a bit of a confrontation with him."

John Wilensky nodded. "Good. Now we have established that this is Weller's gang. Here's my plan of action. You three fellows move around the camp until we have them surrounded on all sides. I'll stay here with the Hardys. When I blow my whistle, we'll all charge. Remember, we know that at least one gang member is missing since Frank was attacked by four people. There may be more in the cabin. Don't take any unnecessary chances."

When the three FBI men were gone, John Wilensky turned to the Hardys. "The same orders as before still apply. Stay behind and out of sight until I tell you everything's safe."

"Where is Ace, though?" Joe asked.

"In the cabin, perhaps. After the fight he gave them, I don't suppose they'll let him run around by himself. Now get back. My men will be ready any second."

Frank and Joe did as they were told. They had just returned to their position when the whistle blew. As the government men charged, Frank and Joe moved up to the edge of the ridge. When they got there, Weller and his henchmen had their hands in the air, covered by Wilensky and two agents. A third agent came out of the cabin.

"There's nobody in here," he reported.

Wilensky looked up at the ridge. "Frank! Joe! You can come here now."

They needed no second bidding. As Frank came near, he glared at one of the gangsters. "You're the one who slugged me!"

The man squirmed nervously. "I thought you was part of Camor's mob, kid. I'd never have hit you if I knew you were on Ace's side."

"Assault can be added to kidnapping," John Wilensky said.

"Kidnapping?" Weller was outraged as he came out of the water. "How stupid can you government people be? We didn't kidnap Ace. We brought him here for his own protection."

"His own protection?" the FBI man challenged. "We heard you dragging him away kicking and screaming. That doesn't sound like he was anxious to go with you."

The gambler smiled sheepishly. "You know how it is with kids sometimes. At first, they don't know what's good for them. Later on, though, they're grateful."

"And Ace is grateful, huh? We'll see what he has to say about that. Where is he?"

"He went out running about ten minutes ago. He has to keep in shape, you know."

Frank was incredulous. "He's out running alone?"

Weller fidgeted. "Well—not exactly alone. I sent one of my men with him to see he doesn't get hurt or attacked by a bear or something. Look, I've got a lot of money riding on that game on Saturday and Ace is my ace in the hole."

"Your concern for his health is very touching," Wilensky said dryly. "But I can't see why you had to snatch him. You had practically wiped out Camor and he's now in jail."

"How do I know if there aren't other guys out to hurt the kid?"

The FBI man shook his head. "Your logic is astounding. Incidently, how did you know where Sureshot was hiding out?"

Weller had a smug expression on his face. "Oh, I had a spy in his gang. He phoned me last night to tell me Camor was at the Moonrise. Then he talked the other guys into deserting. That wasn't hard to do because Camor was acting like a loser, and no one wants to be connected with a loser. Look, you people shouldn't be bugging me. I went to a lot of trouble to help

Ace. Actually, I was going to bring him up here myself for protection when Camor kidnapped him. But he's now free as the wind. As a matter of fact, running was his own idea. To tell the truth, I'm glad you showed up."

John Wilensky was amused at this fast-talking crook. "Just why are you glad we came?"

"You should know. I've had the responsibility of protecting him. Now you're taking over the job and I can go back to New York—after I've had a few days of fishing, of course."

Wilensky laughed. "Weller, you really slay me. In the first place, we're not taking over the job of protecting Ace. He can do that very well by himself as long as he doesn't have guys like you bothering him. When you go to New York, you'll be in handcuffs; the government doesn't look upon you as a helpful partner. And I'm afraid you won't be able to fish for many years. I don't know any federal penitentiary that has streams like this running through it."

Weller's face was a mixture of sadness and shock. "That's gratitude for you!"

"Why don't we go look for Ace?" Joe asked.

"Two reasons," Wilensky said. "We don't know how Ace's guard might react if we came upon them in the woods. He might start shooting. Second, we don't know where they are."

"But won't that guy pull a gun when he sees us all here? Frank asked.

"With six of us here and his friends disarmed? I doubt it. Chances are he'll take off for the hills."

Weller snorted. "He's not carrying a rod. Hey, FBI man, did you ever try to jog with a gun in your belt?"

Just then a man staggered out of the woods. "Boss, Ace got—"

Then he saw the FBI men and the Hardys. He turned and started to run back into the trees, but he was too exhausted to move more than a few steps. One of the agents easily caught up and led the crook back to Wilensky.

"Where is Ace?"

"He . . . he got away. I just couldn't . . . keep up. He was . . . too fast."

11 Lost In A Blizzard

Wilensky sprang into action. The five kidnappers were handcuffed and shoved into their cars. "We'll get a search party together in town as soon as we get these birds locked up," the FBI man explained.

Weller kept wailing as they were driven to Calaboo. "Let us help. You can use us. I've got a big stake in that kid. He's got to make that game Saturday."

"Is that all you're interested in?" Joe asked. "If he wasn't a great football player, would you be so interested in his safety?"

Weller looked hurt. "I ain't made of stone. I got a heart, too. Only business is business. You got to remember, if he wasn't a football star, he wouldn't be here."

"That's right. He'd be at the university all safe and sound," Frank pointed out.

Weller shook his head. "Ace never should have run away. He should have remembered I was his friend."

"One of his close buddies," Joe said, but the gambler missed the sarcasm.

When they reached the village, John Wilensky rushed for a phone. He called the state police and the forest rangers. Mr. Potts gathered together a number of local guides, and within an hour, a large search party had assembled in the town square.

"All right, men," John Wilensky shouted, "you all know what you have to do. We're going to Caleb Hutchinson's cabin. There we'll fan out."

Frank and Joe had brought boots, heavy socks, an extra sweater each, caps, mufflers, and gloves. "Now I feel prepared," Joe said.

As the party was getting into their cars, Mr. Potts came running out of his store. "I thought you'd like to know that a late fall cold snap is coming fast from the west accompanied by snow, according to the radio."

"Thanks," said the agent. "That makes it

more urgent that we find Ace quickly."

Once back at the cabin, the searchers were split up into groups of two and went off in different directions. Frank and Joe walked due east where Ace's guard had come from.

There was a trail so narrow that they had to walk in single file. They assumed that Ace and the guard had run along it. But at what point had Ace escaped?

"What direction did he go in?" Joe wondered aloud.

"It's all guesswork," Frank said.

Each group of the search party had been given a radio. The one in Frank's pocket crackled. "Group fourteen, come in, please," came John Wilensky's voice from his command post back at the cabin.

Frank held the speaker up to his mouth and pushed a button. "Group fourteen reporting."

"Joe and Frank, we're just checking on the reception. You're coming in loud and clear. Please call in every half-hour or so and report immediately if you find Ace or anything that might tell us the direction he went in."

"Will do," Frank said and put the radio back into his pocket.

A cold wind began to blow at their backs. Above them, gray clouds raced eastward. They pulled their jacket zippers up to their necks. "I just hope that snow holds off," Joe said.

It was a futile wish. Before they had gone another mile, flakes fell on their faces, cold and stinging.

"He couldn't have gone much farther than this before he escaped," Frank theorized. "Weller said he had left only ten minutes before the guard returned, and even a fast runner can't do more than a couple of miles in that time. But did he go right or left?"

"What'll we do, flip a coin?"

"I can't get my hand in my pocket without taking my gloves off, and it's too cold for that," Frank replied. "Suppose we turn to the right. That's south and toward the road. Ace may have tried that."

They pushed into the woods. Frank switched on the radio. "Group fourteen reporting."

"Yes, Frank," said the FBI man.

"We're turning south into the woods about two and a half miles down the trail, Mr. Wilensky."

"Okay. We're marking you on the map. Keep in touch."

It was much darker under the trees and the shadows fooled them continually. They often thought they saw Ace, but it turned out to be a bush or a log. They shouted his name, but the wind was howling by this time. The snow came in clumps and they had to keep rubbing it out of their eyes. It massed on the ground and made walking difficult.

They were freezing despite the fact that they were dressed warmly, but it never occurred to them to stop. The end of the afternoon was drawing near and the faint light was fading fast. The young men did not talk, but both felt each other's despair. Ace had been out for several hours. He had been exposed to the freezing wind and snow, still dressed, as far as they knew, in the light clothes he had been wearing the previous night. Besides, he had been beaten, tied up for a period, and he had little if any sleep.

All these factors added up to one horrifying conclusion: every minute out in this weather meant his chances for survival were getting dimmer and dimmer.

Suddenly, they heard a low cry as the howling of the wind abated for a moment. Straining their eyes, they forged ahead. As they trudged on, they thought they saw Ace leaning against a tree.

Frank and Joe shared a common thought: is it really Ace or another illusion, another bush or log? They kept on yelling as they approached.

"It's . . . he's waving!" Joe yelled joyfully.

About twenty yards in front of them, Ace was standing with his arms raised as if to greet his rescuers. But suddenly they saw him fall! They pushed on as fast as they could, and moments later leaned over him, calling his name. Ace did not respond.

Desperately, they lifted the football star to his feet. Ordinarily, they could have easily carried Ace, but now he was a heavy 196 pounds, and they were exhausted and numb from their exertions and the cold.

Frank took the radio from his pocket. "I don't know what we'd do without this." He turned it on. "Mr. Wilensky, Mr. Wilensky. Group fourteen reporting. We've found Ace! Come in, please, come in. We've found Ace about two miles south of the trail."

There was no answer.

Frank shook the radio and tried again. All was silent. He looked at Joe and sighed. "We'll have to retrace our steps."

But that was impossible. The snow had wiped out their footprints. They looked around wildly, trying to find some clue that would show them the way back to the cabin. But nothing was familiar.

They were lost!

12 Trapped!

"What'll we do?" Joe asked, his teeth chattering from the cold.

"We'll have to get him warm real quick or he'll get hypothermia," Frank said. "A couple of minutes ago, we passed a rock outcropping which would make a good protective shelter. We'll have to shield it from the wind on the one side, but we can make a fire against the rock wall to get some warmth."

"That's a good idea," Joe said. "I have extra matches."

The two boys dragged the exhausted but now conscious football player to the spot Frank had indicated, and while the older Hardy held Ace close to him, Joe gathered large branches and protected their little cave. Then he took over with Ace while Frank collected firewood and started a fire. Every time he bent over, it felt as if a dozen hot pins were digging into his frozen muscles. He was relieved a few minutes later when the fire was started and the Hardys huddled in the cave, Ace in between them. The football player was becoming incoherent and shivering violently.

"We've got to keep him awake!" Frank said. "Otherwise he'll be dead soon!"

The boys opened their jackets and pulled them around their friend, talking to him all the time to make sure that Ace did not go to sleep.

Suddenly, out of the swirl of snow came four shadowy figures—John Wilensky and three other men. The wind was howling so loudly that words could barely be heard, but the rescuers communicated with each other by hand signals. They quickly put blankets around Ace.

"It's a good thing we're not far from the road," one of them shouted. "The ambulance is close by."

They carried the athlete out of the cave, and the Hardys followed. Within ten minutes, they were all in the ambulance. Two medics worked on Ace while Wilensky, out of the sound of the wind, was able to speak to Frank and Joe.

"We've been looking for you for quite a while," he said. "When I couldn't get you by radio, I figured something had gone wrong. The other searchers had come back by that time. They are good trackers but they couldn't find a sign of Ace. So you were our last chance. It was a close call." He glanced soberly at Ace. "Maybe too close for him."

When they arrived at the hospital, Ace was rushed to the emergency ward. Frank, Joe, and John Wilensky spent an anxious hour pacing up and down the waiting room. At last, a doctor came in wearing a broad smile.

"He'll make it," he announced gleefully. "Apparently, there will be almost no frostbite. If he had arrived an hour later, I just don't know. He's sleeping right now. If you fellows want to wait for him to wake up, be my guest. He's being put in room 149."

"Thanks, Doc," Wilensky said, then turned to Frank and Joe. "You two go ahead. I'll be with you in a few minutes. I'm going to phone in my report."

The boys sat next to Ace's bed and watched his peaceful face. They had forgotten most of their own pain. After they drank steaming hot cocoa that a nurse brought in, contentment surged within them.

This bliss was broken by the sudden ring of the phone by the bed. Joe looked at Frank, who shrugged. "Someone obviously dialed the wrong number," he said, picking up the phone.

"I would like to speak to Frank or Joe Hardy, please," came an unmistakable voice.

"This is Frank, Dr. Catello," the boy answered.

"How are you?" the college president asked. "I understand you went through quite an ordeal today."

"We're all right, sir," Frank answered. "Thank you for your concern. We're sitting by Ace's bed. He's sleeping right now, but he looks pretty good."

"Yes, yes, I've been speaking to the doctor in charge and the prognosis is excellent." There was a long pause, and for a fleeting moment, Frank thought that Dr. Catello had hung up. "Frank, the FBI agent—"

"John Wilensky?"

"That's his name. He called Police Chief Higgins, who, in turn, phoned me with the news of Harrington's rescue and your part in it. Chief Higgins spoke to me in somewhat strong terms concerning my treatment of you."

"I'm sorry, sir. I understand how you felt and we—"

"No, no, the chief was quite right. I overreacted and moved too hastily. I had no right to do so. I want to apologize to you and your brother for my conduct. I do hope you accept this. I know that the case is over, but I would like to extend to you, on behalf of the university, an invitation to remain in the room you have been occupying and to attend the Northern game as our guests."

Frank glanced at Joe, who had been listening. The younger brother nodded vigorously.

"That's very kind of you, President Catello. We both accept with many thanks. By the way, Ace is in hot water with the NCAA. What do you think is going to happen?"

"I personally will deal with the NCAA the first thing in the morning," Catello said in a grim voice. "Also with the arrogant young reporter who so viciously attacked Ace." His tone lightened. "When you return, Frank, could you drop by my office at your convenience to give me a full report? I received only sketchy information."

"I'll be happy to."

"Please extend my heartfelt thanks to your brother. And tell Ace when he wakes that the entire student body rejoices at his rescue and the recovery which we trust will be rapid."

"Well, what do you think about that?" Frank

said when he put down the receiver.

"I have to admit I was pretty mad at him," Joe said, "but it takes a big guy to say he was wrong."

Suddenly, the hospital room seemed to bustle with activity. John Wilensky and the attending doctor walked into the room just as Ace woke up.

"Where am I?" the football player focused on Frank.

"The hospital."

He nodded. "I remember seeing you and Joe through kind of a cold fog. I was falling and falling and—" Alarm spread over his face. "Where's Bill? They left him with Camor!" He tried to rise. "I've got to get him!"

The doctor pushed him back gently. "Careful, son. You've been through a terrible experience physically."

"Bill's safe," Joe said quickly. "We took him to President Catello's house. He's being well taken care of."

"Then Catello knows. Bill will have to go back to Chicago!" Ace cried out in alarm.

"Not on your life," Joe said. "President Catello's trying to find a home for him near the university."

"Wow!" Ace thought for a moment. "I guess I

should have gone to him in the first place. Now you know why I wouldn't let anyone look into my room. Bill was there. I'm sorry I acted so stupidly with you fellows, but you know how it is. My father and Bill are all I've got, and my dad's just so helpless now."

"You did what you thought was best," Frank said.

The doctor checked Ace's pulse, temperature, and other vital signs. He finally stood back, smiling. "I don't know how you did it," he said. "You're an amazing specimen of the human race. You're improving minute by minute. Well, I have to be on my rounds. I'll return in about an hour."

After he had gone, Ace said, "It's all beginning to come back to me now. You guys found me, didn't you?"

"That's right," Frank said. "But you really owe it all to Mr. Wilensky here. He's an FBI agent and he worked fast with other agents to expose the Weller gang."

John Wilensky came forward and shook hands with the patient. He then went over what had happened since Harry Weller's goons grabbed Ace in the Moonrise Motel.

Ace grinned. "Hey, you know people usually

get kidnapped *once*. I got kidnapped *twice*! That's some dubious honor, isn't it?"

They all chatted until Ace looked tired again. His visitors said good-bye and went out into the corridor.

"The doctor has set aside a room for you two," John Wilensky told the Hardys. "I'm driving to Berlin and taking a plane home."

"Joe, why don't *you* stay here with Ace?" Frank suggested. "You can come back with him. I'll go with Mr. Wilensky tonight. I feel I ought to report to President Catello as soon as possible."

"I'd be glad to have company," the FBI man said.

"It's all right with me," Joe said, yawning. "As a matter of fact, after I get a bite to eat, I'm going to bed. I'm tired."

The trip to Berlin, New Hampshire, was leisurely. "We've been running so fast since this morning," Wilensky said, "that I think we shouldn't rush now."

They ate a large dinner in a restaurant and then got on the chartered plane. The snowstorm had passed over by this time. The sky was clear and full of stars and a crescent moon. Frank was so hypnotized by the peaceful scene that he was startled when the pilot said, "Seat belts, please. We're preparing to land."

John Wilensky drove Frank back to the FBI office. As the older Hardy brother got into his car, he could hardly believe he had left the vehicle there only fourteen hours before.

The clock in the administration building steeple was striking midnight as Frank walked across the campus. He was whistling as he came into the dormitory and down the hall. He stepped into his room and was grabbed by strong hands in an unbreakable grip!

"Hold him, Scrabby!" Meeb's voice came from beside the door. The door closed and the light was switched on.

Meeb scampered around until he faced Frank. "We've been waiting a long time for you, Hardy. In fact, we were beginning to lose hope. Another few minutes and we would have been gone. Lucky for us, eh? Now, let's talk business. Where is it?"

Scrabby's grip was torture. "What . . . are you . . . talking about?" Frank asked, his eyes becoming blurry.

"Ease up, Scrabby," Meeb said sharply. Immediately, the pressure lessened. "We'll get no information from an unconscious man. Now, my friend, you know exactly what we are talking about. We are speaking of"—his voice lowered—"the bug. I need not say anything more than that, do I?"

"I still don't have the slightest idea of what you're after."

Meeb's eyes rolled toward the ceiling. "He still doesn't have any idea what we're after!" he said. Then he glared at Frank. "Oh, you're very clever, Hardy, very clever indeed." He brought his face up to the youth's. "The gold bug!"

Frank shrugged.

Meeb walked around the room, shaking his fist in the air.

"Do you want me to punish him a little, Mr. Meeb?" Scrabby rumbled.

"I don't know. Actually, I'd rather drag this out for a while . . . kind of make him squirm. A little psychological pressure might do the trick. Let's take him to our house."

Propelled by Scrabby, who had a firm hold on his wrist, Frank was led quickly to the parking lot and shoved into the front seat of a car. Flanked by Meeb and Scrabby, Frank found himself unable to move.

In five minutes, they were in a rundown section of the community. Meeb pulled smoothly to the curb in front of a deserted building. "It may look like a wreck to you, Hardy, but it's a palace to me. You see, I own it and I use it as my administration building." He chuckled. "Bring him along, Scrabby."

Once inside, Meeb turned on a flashlight to reveal a dusty and cobwebbed hall. The small man turned to Frank. "You still don't want to tell us where you hid the bug that Robbie Stevenson gave you?"

"I wouldn't even if I could," Frank retorted defiantly.

Meeb opened a door. "Too bad," he murmured. "You could have saved yourself so much unnecessary trouble. We will win in the end, you know. I always win. Go ahead, Scrabby."

Frank was thrust forward and fell down a flight of stairs, landing in the basement. Meeb's croaky voice floated after him, "You will stay down there, Hardy, without food or water until you tell me what I wish to know."

13 *Lucky Rescue*

The door locked shut and a bolt was slid into place. Frank was left in absolute darkness, hearing only the scratchy sounds of rats scampering across the cement floor.

He got up, gently kneading his aching limbs. Then he walked slowly along the walls, feeling for a door or a window. Twice he fell over debris. There was no opening at all.

Frustrated, he sat on the steps, wondering when Meeb and Scrabby would return. They were his only chance for escape and not much of one at that. Maybe he could tell them that he put the bug in a bank safe and that they could not touch it unless he went with them. Perhaps there would be a possibility of getting away.

He was trying to decide on an appropriate bank when the door opened. "Hey, mister down there," came a quavery voice.

"I'm here," Frank said. "What do you want?"

"Come on up."

Frank proceeded up the stairs cautiously, his fists ready. Who was this? Could the crooks have another partner he hadn't heard about?

"Who are you?" Frank asked.

"Come out in the hall," the stranger said peevishly. "I don't want to stay here too long."

Frank stepped out. He still couldn't see the man, but his instincts told him that the stranger meant him no harm.

"Are you okay?" the man asked.

"I am," Frank said.

"That's good. Well, I'll be going."

Frank reached out toward the voice and found a shoulder to hold.

"Hey, let me go. Don't hurt me," the man protested.

"I'm not going to hurt you. I'm really grateful that you let me out. I just want to know who you are and why you did it."

"My name don't make no difference," his benefactor said. "I don't remember it most of the time, anyhow. I'm nobody important. I've been staying in this building for the last few nights. I heard those guys come in—Meeb and Scrabby. They're a couple of no goods, they are—and I heard the things Meeb said to you. I've known Meeb since he was a kid and he was always rotten. So I decided to get you out of here. But they'll know somebody heard them and search the building. I can't let 'em find me. They caught me the other night and threatened me until I promised I wouldn't go near this place no more."

"Well, I certainly want to thank you," Frank said.

"*Okay, Okay,*" the man said in an annoyed tone. "So let me go now."

Frank released his hold and heard the man shuffle toward the front door. When it opened, the young detective saw his rescuer framed in the light. He was middle aged, crippled, and bent over.

Frank started after him. The vagrant had only gone a few steps, though, when he let out a blood-curdling shriek. Scrabby had slipped out of a nearby doorway and was squeezing the back of the unfortunate man's neck.

Frank immediately jumped on Scrabby's back, and the surprised giant let go his hold on the vagrant's neck. He turned his attention to Frank as the crippled man disappeared down an alley.

A huge arm came around and grabbed Frank, pulling him over the criminal's shoulder. "You!" Scrabby yelled. He took Frank's arm and held it in his terrible vise. "I thought I would come to check everything out. And look what I caught!"

The pain was excruciating and Frank knew if he didn't act quickly, he would pass out. With all the strength he could muster, he delivered a well-aimed kick to Scrabby's ankle. The gigantic man howled and dropped his hand to grab his leg. Frank began to run.

"You come back here," Scrabby yelled. Frank shot a glance over his shoulder and saw that the giant had taken a few steps in his pursuit. But he was no match for Frank, and a block away, the young detective found a taxi. Within ten minutes, he was back on campus.

Approaching the dormitory, he bumped into Pops Walzak. "You don't look too well, lad," the head of the campus police said. "What happened?"

Frank told him the events of the seemingly endless day—the flight to New York and then to New Hampshire, capturing Weller and his gang, the blizzard, the rush to the hospital, Meeb and Scrabby, the rat-infested basement, and his subsequent rescue.

"You had more adventures in a day than most people have in a lifetime," Walzak commented.

"I'm worried that Scrabby will return to our room tonight," Frank said thoughtfully.

"You mean this morning," Walzak gently kidded him. "But why don't you use Ace's room? I'm sure it will be all right," he added. I'll have a man pass through the hall every hour."

"Thanks, Pops."

But the rest of the night was peaceful. Frank slept until eight, then showered and had a hearty breakfast at the campus cafeteria. At nine-thirty, he went to President Catello's office and reported Ace's rescue.

"So it's all over," the beaming administrator said, "at long last. Now affairs can return to normal."

"I hope so, sir, but I have this feeling that there may be more," Frank said. "It isn't something I can put my finger on, but I don't think Ace is out of trouble yet!"

"What does the Bible say?" Catello said, rising and coming to the other side of the desk. 'Sufficient unto the day is the evil thereof.' In other words, don't worry about what might happen tomorrow because it might not happen at all. What you need is some more rest. You still look haggard."

Frank thought the last statement was exaggerated until he looked in a mirror back in Ace's room. I really am a wreck, he said to himself. He lay down on Ace's bed and was asleep in a moment.

He slept until Joe and Ace burst into the room. "Hey, you bum, are you going to lie there all day?" Ace laughed. He and Joe tumbled Frank onto the floor.

"It's two o'clock!" Joe said.

"I was out like a light," Frank admitted, "but now I'm raring to go!" He threw a pillow and hit his brother.

Moments later, their playful fight was interrupted by a crowd of students outside yelling, "Ace, Ace, Ace!"

"What's all that about?" Frank asked.

"They were waiting at the airport," Joe said. They followed us all the way here. I guess you heard about the NCAA."

"No, what?"

"It lifted all the restrictions on the university. Also that reporter Cliff Moorson made a public apology to Ace."

Frank buttoned his shirt. "He never should have made those remarks in the first place! Ace, how do you feel?"

"Like a million bucks," the athlete said, shadow boxing with himself in the mirror.

"The doctor said an average person would have had to stay in bed a month." Joe chuckled. "A good athlete needs a week of recuperation. But Ace will be back to normal in a day or two."

"Come on," Ace said. "Bill is still over at the Catellos' and I want to see him. Then I'm going to the stadium. The team doctor has to check me out, but that will only be a formality."

"Why don't you go along with him, Joe?" Frank suggested. "I want to see how Robbie is doing at the hospital."

"Okay." Joe and Ace left. Frank finished dressing, walked out to the street, and hailed a cab. In ten minutes, he was at the hospital desk.

"I'm sorry, but you cannot see Robert Stevenson," a nurse informed Frank. "His mother has left instructions that no one—absolutely no one—is to be admitted without her permission."

"Well, can you tell me how he is doing?"

"Oh, yes. He is recovering at a good rate, but it will be a couple of days before he'll return home."

"Thank you," Frank said and left. He was puzzled. He could understand Mrs. Stevenson's concern, but her stubborn attitude seemed uncalled for.

He joined Joe and Ace at the stadium. The athlete's mood had reversed itself. He was grim and angry. "The doc won't let me play today. Maybe tomorrow, he says."

"Ace, listen to reason," Frank said. "In the last few days, you were pushed off the library steps, almost hit by a car, knocked down by a blackjack, fought with a group of men, got lost in the woods, and nearly froze to death. Now, if you were the doctor, don't you think you might have some doubts?"

"I say amen to that." Coach Bradley had overheard Frank as he joined them. "Look, I want you to be ready for the Northern game, son. And I'm not taking any chances on losing you this afternoon in a scrimmage. It's bad enough losing Tank—what a loser he turned out to be!—but to lose you, too, would be a disaster. We would have to send Northern a white flag."

"Oh, I know you're right," the quarterback grumbled, "but it doesn't make me feel any better. Well, if I can't practice this afternoon, I'm not going to stay here and watch it."

He turned on his heel and left, followed by Joe and Frank. As they went through the locker room door, Joe said, "Uh-oh." It was their misfortune to find themselves in the midst of the SAPA picketers. There were only ten of them this time and, as before, they were led by Carol Crider.

It was the wrong time to challenge Ace. "Get out of my way," he growled.

She met his glare with a sweet smile. "We of SAPA are happy that you have survived such an ordeal. We do want to point out, though, that this does not change our mind about athletic scholarships."

"Who cares?" he retorted. Ace attempting to move around her, but she kept on getting in his way.

She put her hands on her hips and frowned at him. "That's very rude! But skip that. You're intelligent; in fact, you're a top student. You must surely see how destructive the system is to some deserving students. Now we beg of you to publicly denounce and expose the scholarship program for athletes. Coming from you, it would be—"

He held up his hand. "Hold it! *You* want *me* to say to everyone that sports and truly talented athletes are not deserving of financial backing? Is that it?"

"That's right," she said brightly. "You have the idea."

"Then you are out of your mind. What makes you think for one second that I would do such a crazy thing? A solid sports program develops strong and important qualities in students. And that goes for the spectators as well as the athletes."

He moved past her, as she angrily clenched her fists.

Ace walked quickly for a while. Then his pace grew slower and slower as he relaxed. At last, he chuckled. "I guess she really believes what she is saying. You can't blame her for that. Too bad. She's probably the most unpopular person on campus right now and in all likelihood doesn't know why. She's too busy fighting for what she believes in. You have to admire that though, I must admit."

To their amazement, Frank and Joe noticed a smile on his face. "She's a good-looking girl, too!"

Ace stopped in front of the library. "I've got some research to do for a term paper. Do you want to come in with me? I may be here as long as two hours."

Frank and Joe nodded. "Sure."

The boys had been doing chemical experiments in their laboratory at home, but had hesitated to continue them because they weren't sure what results further steps might bring, so while Ace studied, they immersed themselves in chemistry books. They were still pouring over them when their friend joined them two hours later.

"I've never seen anybody working as hard as you," Ace teased as he helped them put away the mountain of texts.

Joe grinned. "It was fun!"

They were passing the front desk when they saw a women going out a side door marked LIBRARY PERSONNEL ONLY. She paused and called to the checkout clerk, "Good night, Johnny."

"Good night, Mrs. Stevenson," he called back. Then she went through the door.

Frank and Joe stopped. "That's Robbie's mother!"

"What's she doing here?" Frank asked.

"Why wouldn't she be here? She's the director," Ace spoke up.

"The director of the library?

"Right. Why are you guys so interested in her, anyhow?"

They told him how they had met Robbie and how Scrabby and Meeb had threatened him and eventually sent him to the hospital. Then

Frank told of his adventure in the basement with the rats the night before.

"How come you didn't say anything about this before?" Joe asked.

"There's been no time."

"If I get hold of those guys, they'll be sorry," Ace said, doubling his hands. "I never met Robbie, but I think I've seen him a couple of times."

The Hardys looked at him. They said nothing, but both wondered how long even Ace could last against the giant.

"Ace, wait!"

The athlete turned. Professor Overton came up to them, puffing. "It's wonderful to see you," he said. "Of course, I've heard all about your narrow escape. I thought for a while I was going to lose my prize student."

"I thought so, too." Ace grinned ruefully.

"Well, as a celebration, we must have dinner together, all four of us. No, no, don't protest, this is my treat."

Overton took the young people to an expensive restaurant in town where they had thick steaks. As they relaxed, the professor said, "I'm sorry the team doctor won't give you the green light yet, Ace, but at least you are alive. I imagine you are very grateful for that. Also, I know

127

that years from now when you are a leading physicist, you will see football for what it is—a silly game. Even if you miss Saturday's event, it will not be the terrible tragedy you think it is."

Ace did not reply.

They were walking across the street back to campus when he asked, "Have you looked over my last paper yet, Professor? I'm curious about what you think of the formula."

The scholar staggered and clutched his head. The youths grabbed him before he fell.

"Are you all right, sir?" Ace cried, alarmed.

Overton took a deep breath. "I'm fine now, I think. I suddenly get these tremendous and agonizing headaches. Please don't tell anyone about this attack. I dislike people worrying about me."

"You ought to see a doctor," Frank suggested.

"Oh, I will, I will. Anyway, I must go now. I'll see you fellows tomorrow."

With that, he parted from the group and walked in the direction of his apartment.

The trio watched him. "Thanks for the dinner," they called after him, then they went to Ace's room. At the door, they stopped.

"Well, back to the books for me," the football player declared.

"At least you won't have to go out for groceries tonight," Frank pointed out.

Ace laughed and went into his room. Frank and Joe were just unlocking their door when they heard the shattering of glass and a thud.

Ace opened his door again, his face white. "Come and see what's happened now!" he cried.

The boys ran in. One of the windows was broken, and stuck in the wall opposite it was an arrow!

14 Carol Is Accused

Frank and Joe turned, dashed down the hall, and ran outside. "There," Frank shouted, pointing toward a clump of trees.

Before they got there, Carol Crider stepped out of the shadows, holding an arrow. She looked at them with a puzzled expression. "What is this all about?"

At that moment, Pops Walzak arrived. "I heard glass shattering. Do you know anything about it?"

Joe pointed to the broken window. "Someone took a shot at Ace with an arrow."

The campus guard groaned. "Not again!" Then he saw the arrow in Carol's hand. "You?"

By this time, Ace had joined them. He shook his head. "Not a chance. She wouldn't do that."

"I think we ought to go inside and talk this over," said Pops. He led the way to Ace's room. "Now, exactly what happened?"

Ace said he had been standing and stretching. Then, as he moved to sit down at his desk, he heard the window break and the sound of the arrow hitting the wall. "If I had kept on stretching, I would have been hit!" He shivered a little in spite of his usual stoic attitude.

"Now it's your turn, Ms. Crider," Pops said. "How come you were outside the window?"

"I was returning from the library. I live over in Hawkshaw Hall and that path in back of this building is the shortest way to my room."

"It makes a lot of sense to me," Ace said. "There's nothing sinister in that."

Walzak gave him a sharp look, but said gently, "Suppose we let Ms. Crider tell it in her own words."

The athlete raised his hands in surrender. "Anything you say, Pops."

"Anyway," Carol continued, "I was approaching that group of trees when I heard a whizzing and then the glass breaking. I could see someone in the shadow of the trees and shouted, 'What are you doing?'"

"That was pretty brave of you," Ace commented.

"Please, this is not a courtroom," said Pops in exasperation, "and you're not on the witness stand testifying to her good character. Ms. Crider, did anyone hear you call? Besides the person you saw, I mean?"

Carol thought. "Maybe, but I didn't notice anyone else. Anyhow, the man panicked—"

"Are you sure it was a man?"

"Pretty sure. It was dark, of course, and I didn't get a good look at him. When I yelled, he ran. I saw that he dropped something so I went over and found this arrow. That's when these fellows came out," she pointed at Frank and Joe. "You know the rest."

"Could I please have the arrow?" Pops requested. She passed it to him. "I must tell you that I find your story rather flimsy. You talk about a man whom no one else saw. It is true that you would come this way from the library. On the other hand, I heard this afternoon that you were very angry with Ace. You are the head of an organization which hates all that he stands for."

The young woman was shocked. She said in a low voice, "That's absurd. I . . . I wouldn't do anything violent."

"Of course, it's absurd," Ace broke in. "I said some things, too, that weren't too nice."

"But you didn't shoot an arrow through her window, did you? I'm going to phone the police. You three guard her until I get back."

"Are you sure you can trust us?" Ace grinned. "I mean, she might overpower us at any moment, tie us up, and run away."

"Wise guy!" Pops Walzak grumbled on his way out.

Two hours later, Ace, Frank, and Joe talked to Chief Higgins at police headquarters. Carol had been named a prime suspect pending investigation.

"This is so ridiculous," Ace grumbled. "She didn't do it."

Frank shot a glance at his friend. "You seem mighty sure."

"I am. I believe her story. After all, where's the bow?"

Chief Higgins smiled. "That's true, but it's probably in the clump of trees where she threw it. We'll find it in the morning. Speaking of morning, don't touch the arrow in the wall or disturb it in any way. A police expert will arrive bright and early to look it over. And don't mention the incident to anyone."

"Why don't you sleep in our room tonight?" Frank suggested when they got back to the dorm. "If your theory is right about Carol being innocent, then the real would-be killer might return."

"Thanks," Ace said. "I can bring the cot I've been sleeping on since Bill arrived."

As they set up the cot, Joe teased, "You seem to like her."

"Who? Oh, you mean Carol Crider." The Hardys saw the football star's cheeks turn red. "I just don't want to see her framed, that's all. I'd feel that way about anybody in the same spot."

They continued to stare at him and he looked a little sheepish. "Well, maybe I like her some. I mean, she's good looking and has brains and a lot of guts, although her ideas are crazy."

Five minutes later, the three young men were asleep.

About midnight, the door crashed open as a massive body smashed against it, tearing out the lock.

"Where is it?" Scrabby yelled as he grabbed Frank, whose bed was nearest to the door. "The kid said you had it!"

He was choking Frank when Joe jumped on him. Ace reacted a bit slower. He sat up and rubbed his eyes, then, seeing his friends in a fight, he leaped to their defense.

Scrabby released Frank to battle his new adversaries. He flung Joe across the room, but was tackled by Ace and hit in the face by Frank. Joe returned quickly, butting the giant in the stomach with his head. The huge bully retreated to the hallway as blows rained upon him. Suddenly, he turned and ran. The Hardys and Ace would have followed, but Scrabby's fists had also taken their toll. They all leaned against the wall to regain their breath and strength.

"You have the strangest friends," Ace said after he stopped panting. "Our team wouldn't need a line if we had him. Who is he, anyhow?"

"You have just been introduced to Scrabby," Joe said.

"That's the cockroach who beat up that boy Robbie? Whew! I thought you were exaggerating when you told me about this creep, but you weren't telling half. He's something!"

"Yes," Frank said. "But he'll fight only when the odds are on his side. Faced with real opposition—he runs."

"Then I won't recommend him to Coach Bradley," Ace said. "Where do you suggest we sleep for the rest of the night? In a bank vault?"

Frank laughed. "I don't think that will be necessary. He won't be back now that he's been beaten."

He was right. They all rested well, skipping their early morning run. When Ace and Joe woke at eight-thirty, they found that Frank was gone.

He returned when they had finished dressing. "Where have you been?" Joe asked. "We thought you might have been kidnapped by Scrabby and Meeb again!"

"Oh, you know better than that. I got up early to look at that arrow. I had a theory, but I had to go to the library to confirm it."

"Don't keep us waiting," Ace said. "What is it?"

"Part of the proof that Carol couldn't have shot that arrow!"

They gaped at him. "No kidding?" Ace exclaimed.

"It looked strange to me," Frank went on, "shorter than the ones you see in archery matches. Actually, it's *quarrel*, that is, made for a crossbow."

Joe nodded, understanding what his brother was getting at. "A crossbow takes a lot of power to pull back. Carol doesn't look like a weakling, but I don't think she could do it."

"Hey, that's great!" Ace pounded Frank's back until the boy winced. "What's the rest of the proof Carol couldn't have done it?"

"We'll have to conduct an experiment and we need your help."

"You've got it!"

"Okay, let's go." Frank led the way to Ace's room. "Ace, you stand in front of that arrow. Joe and I have to go outside."

The brothers walked to the clump of trees. "Would you say this is where we first saw Carol last night?" Frank asked.

"About a step to your right."

"Good." Frank moved one step. "From here I can just see Ace's head. But Carol isn't as tall as I am."

"She stands slightly below your shoulder," Joe agreed.

Frank bent down. "About here?" He raised his voice. "Ace, are you still standing in front of the arrow?"

"I am."

"I can't see him," Frank said to Joe. "If I can't see him, neither could Carol."

Ace appeared at the broken window. "What did you find?"

Frank told him. "The police claim that she pulled an arrow she couldn't pull to shoot at an

137

object she couldn't see. It just won't hold water."

The police expert who arrived a few minutes later agreed. "Also, we checked that clump of trees at sunup and couldn't find the bow. Oh, and listen, don't discuss the fact that the arrow was shot with a crossbow with anyone around here, until the case is wrapped up, okay?"

"We won't," Frank promised. "Can we tell our father, though?"

"Sure. But don't talk about it around campus."

"Well, I'm glad Carol is proven innocent," Ace declared. "But who shot at me? Camor and Weller are in jail!"

"I haven't got the slightest idea," Frank said, worried.

They went back inside so Ace could get his notebooks for his classes. The boys were almost out of the dormitory when the hall phone rang. Frank picked it up. "I would like to speak to Frank Hardy," a silky, familiar voice said.

"I don't want to talk to you, Meeb." He started to put down the receiver.

"Hear me out, Hardy. It will be worth your while."

Frank reluctantly brought the phone back to his ear. "I'll give you a minute."

"Fair enough. You probably resent my attempt to gain what is rightfully my property. Why don't you let bygones be bygones? After all, you did get out of the basement. You did give my friend Scrabby a very sore ankle. And last night, he informed me that you and an army of friends piled up on him unfairly."

Frank looked with amusement at Ace and Joe. "I wish you would get to the point, Meeb. You didn't phone to tell me how unhappy Scrabby is."

Meeb chuckled. "Very true. I would like to meet with you."

"You have a nerve! Robbie and I ought to swear out warrants for your arrest on charges of assault."

"Now what would be the use of that? What witnesses could you call? Anyway, I would be out on bail within an hour. And I doubt if young Stevenson will agree to your plan. Hardy, let's make sense. You and I have mutual interests."

Frank thought quickly. Meeb, after all, was the key to the mystery. "Where and when shall we meet?"

"Now you're being reasonable. At the Black Coffee Cafeteria—that's at Main and Second Street in town—right now. There are conditions, though."

"Which are?"

"You don't bring the police. I won't bring Scrabby."

"All right." The young detective hung up and related the conversation to Joe and Ace.

"I'd like to go, but I have an economics lecture in fifteen minutes," Ace said.

"Joe, why don't—"

"I know," Joe said resignedly. "Why don't I go with Ace? I'll worry about you meeting that crook alone."

"The Black Coffee Cafeteria sounds like a fairly public place where they can't kidnap me. I'll be careful. They're not going to get me again."

"We'll meet you at the student center," Ace said.

The cafeteria, as Frank thought, was crowded with students eating a late breakfast. Meeb was sitting in the last booth. There was no sign of Scrabby. The small man was drinking coffee and munching on a doughnut.

"Sit down, Hardy. Would you like something? Coffee? Tea? Danish?"

"No," Frank said coldly. "I'm not in the mood for such hospitality. I don't want to stay in your company longer than I have to. Tell me what you want."

"Today's youth just doesn't have any manners," Meeb observed sadly. "All right, I'll put my cards on the table. I'll pay you four thousand dollars for the bug."

"You must be kidding!"

"I see your point. Six thousand."

"I don't believe this. I've told you we don't have any bug."

Meeb waved away that objection. "Let's not go through that again. You have it. Stevenson said you had it. You drive a hard bargain, Hardy. Eight thousand. Think of what you can do with that cash."

"I told you, we don't have it!" Frank stood up.

Meeb's face was convulsed with fury. He shook his fist. "I know what you're trying to do! You want to sell it yourself. Well, you won't get away with it. It was my idea and I deserve the money. I'll get you, Hardy, and you can tell Robbie his mother had better watch out!"

Frank walked out, followed by Meeb's curses.

The young detective joined Ace and Joe at the student center. They all had soft drinks while he related his encounter with Meeb.

"The guy's crazy," Ace said. "Well, I've got to go over to the library for a few minutes."

"Let's go along, Joe," Frank said. "Maybe we'll be able to see Mrs. Stevenson."

They had to talk their way past her secretary, but when they mentioned President Catello, they were admitted into the director's office immediately.

She stood up when they walked in. "You!"

"Take it easy, Mrs. Stevenson," Frank held up a hand. "We're not your enemies."

"I realize that," she said sadly. "Please sit down. Robbie told me you were kind to him and I believe him. I apologize for my behavior."

"We understand," Joe said.

"I wish I knew what was going on," she said. "Robbie's recovering—physically. But he's terrified. He won't say a word as to why he was beaten."

"We don't know exactly why either," Frank said. He told her about Meeb and Scrabby and what they had done. "All we know is that Robbie wants to protect you. They have threatened to hurt you. Because of that, he has stolen something, but he won't give it to them."

She stared at him. "He stole something? What?"

Frank shrugged. "We don't know."

"It's an insect," Joe broke in. "A bug. A gold bug."

Mrs. Stevenson turned pale. "A gold bug," she whispered. "Are you sure?"

They nodded. She was about to say more when the phone rang. She picked it up. "What? Yes, I'll be right there."

She hurried toward the door. "Robbie's left the hospital. He ran away!"

15 Fire!

Frank and Joe followed the distraught woman and offered to drive her to the hospital. There they questioned everyone who had been in contact with Robbie and found out that he was last seen in his room an hour before. Some time later, the receptionist noticed a boy that fitted Robbie's description leave the building. He was not accompanied by anyone.

"What shall I do?" Mrs. Stevenson was beside herself.

"I think you should call the police," Frank advised. "And we'll keep an eye out for Robbie. Maybe he hid on campus somewhere because he's afraid of Meeb and Scrabby."

"We'll do our best to find him," Joe assured the woman. "We just need a clue as to where he could have gone."

Mrs. Stevenson had no ideas to offer, so finally the young detectives drove her back to the library. In all the excitement, they forgot to ask her if the gold bug meant anything to her.

When they went to Ace's room, they found President Catello with their friend. He was inspecting the hole the arrow had made.

"I guess your hunch was right," he said to Frank. "Now you'll have to guard Ace more closely than ever."

"I've been thinking about that," Frank said. "Why don't we take Ace to our house in Bayport at night? He'll be well protected there and no one would know where he is. We can drive him back and forth so he won't miss any classes."

"I think that's an excellent alternative to staying here," Catello said, "but, of course, the final choice is up to Kevin."

Ace grinned. "I'll go for it. The only other choice is for the police to let Harry Weller and his men out of jail and come here to guard me. That guy would never let anything happen to me even if he had to put me in an underground concrete cell—until Saturday, that is. After that, he wouldn't care."

He sobered. "I would not mind getting some sleep for a change. Something has been going on almost every night here. Sure, I'll go."

"Good, good." The president shook hands with the three youths and left. Frank phoned Mrs. Hardy and told her he had invited Ace to their home. She said he would be most welcome.

"Well, off to the laboratory," Ace said.

They walked across the campus. Ace had always been popular, but now he drew twice as much attention as before. Fellow students tried to stop him to chat and wish him luck, but he went by them with a friendly greeting.

"Another terrible experience, eh, Ace?" Professor Overton was standing at the door to the physics laboratory. He stared down at his prize pupil with tired eyes.

"You don't have to worry about me any more, Professor," Ace said breezily. "I'm going to stay at the Hardys for a while."

Overton's eyes sparkled. "Splendid!"

Once more Frank and Joe sat in a corner. For a few minutes, the professor walked around the room, watching his students at work. Then he went to the window where he stood for the next hour, staring out at the sky, oblivious to all that was going on. The bell rang for the end of the period, but he didn't move.

Ace came up to him. "Professor Overton?"

Still the scholar was motionless.

"Sir?" The athlete touched his mentor lightly on the shoulder. "Sir, the period is over."

Overton jumped and turned. "What?"

"Can we go?"

"Go?" the scholar said vaguely. "Oh, yes, go, go."

Ace was worried as they walked toward the stadium. "You know, the professor looked at me as if he didn't know me. I don't think he knew where he was. He's acting very strangely lately."

We've noticed," Frank said.

Once more, Ace went through a physical examination. When he came out of the team doctor's office, he was grinning from ear to ear. "Hey, I passed!" he shouted. "I can suit up for practice." The coach and the entire team broke into cheers.

"I wish you could check on one thing," Ace asked the Hardys. "What's happened with Carol and the arrow deal?"

"We'll call the police," Frank promised. He and Joe went to a pay phone.

"She's still under strong suspicion," Chief Higgins said.

"Didn't the findings of your expert have any weight?" Frank asked.

"They were your findings, too, to be fair about it. Well, they did with me. But the district attorney wants to have a hearing, and he's out of the state today. You saved me a call because he wants you, your brother, and Ace there, too. Tomorrow morning at nine!"

During scrimmage, the Hardys went all over campus asking people if they had seen Robbie. Few knew him, and no one could supply any clues. They called Mrs. Stevenson, who had not heard from her son either.

"Could he have gone to a relative's house?" Frank pressed, "or a friend's?"

"The only relatives we have live in Wisconsin, and I called all his friends," the woman replied. "No one's see him."

Frank was worried about the boy, but he knew there was nothing they could do. After practice was over, they went back to Ace's room so he could pack, then they drove the thirty miles to Bayport.

"Hey, dad's home!" Joe shouted, seeing his father through the window. He was sitting in the living room with Mrs. Hardy and Aunt Gertrude.

After Ace had been introduced and heartily greeted, Fenton Hardy explained his unexpected presence. "I'm back for just a few days.

We thought we had the case all wrapped up, but ran into last minute snags so I've got to check out some files of the New York City Police Department. I had just walked in when President Catello phoned. He wanted to thank us for boarding Ace and, to show his appreciation, he said that there would be tickets at the stadium gate Saturday for your mother, Aunt Gertrude, and me. That was very nice of him." He winked at Ace. "You'll have to put on a show now. After all, we're driving thirty miles to see you."

Ace grinned. "I'll do my best."

"I hope you like roast beef," Aunt Gertrude said. "That's our dinner tonight."

"Ma'am, I've heard Frank and Joe brag so much about your cooking," Ace said, "that I'm sure anything you serve will be delicious."

She gave him a severe look. "I can see that in addition to your athletic skills you have mastered the dubious art of flattery." Despite her sharp remark, everyone knew she was pleased. "Well, since it's ready to take out of the oven, you can test whether my nephews tell the truth," she concluded.

They were on their way into the dining room when the phone rang. Joe went to pick it up. "Hello?"

"Joe, this is Chet," their close friend boomed. "Where have you been? I haven't seen you around for days."

Joe briefly described their duties.

"Right at the college, huh, with Ace Harrington? Are you lucky! Hey, now that you're home, why don't I come over and spend the night? My parents and Iola aren't here anyway, and I'm kind of lonely."

"Just a second," Joe went into the dining room.

"It's all right with me," Mrs. Hardy said. "The more the merrier."

"Maybe he can come back to college with us," Ace offered. "He'd enjoy the rally tomorrow night."

"I'm sure he'd like that," Joe said and returned to the phone. "Chet, if you hurry, you can join us for dinner!"

"I'll be right over!"

The chubby boy arrived when the family was having dessert. "Oh, Aunt Gertrude made my favorite pie!" he cried out. "Save me some while I'm getting rid of that leftover roast beef."

While Chet dug into his dinner with gusto, the family discussed the latest development in the case.

"The last attempt on your life—the one with

the arrow—may have nothing to do with the football game," Mr. Hardy said to Ace.

"I know," the boy replied. "That's what's so hard to deal with. I don't know anyone who would want to harm me."

"Do you think it was Scrabby and Meeb?" Frank asked.

"I doubt it," Joe put in. "They have nothing against Ace. They want Robbie, and Ace doesn't even know the boy. No. It's got to be something else, something Ace isn't even aware of."

"That means it might continue after the Northern game," Ace said gloomily.

"Let's hope not," Fenton Hardy said. "This kind of person will be caught, I'm sure. He or she is too open, acts too oddly—using a quarrel for example. What will it be next time?"

"You mean that arrow was shot with a crossbow?" Chet asked.

Frank nodded. "How did you know?"

"Oh, I've been studying that kind of stuff. There's a lot of interest around the state in weapons of medieval days. There are clubs where they even have tournaments. You know, people dress up in armor, get on horses and charge at each other with lances. The lances are made of rubber so it's pretty hard to get hurt. By the way, one of the best clubs is right near the university."

"That's interesting, Chet," Frank said thoughtfully, but then dropped the subject.

They all watched TV for a while and finally Ace stood up. "I hope none of you mind, but I have to hit the books for a while and then get that sleep I've been promised."

"Your room is at the end of the hall," Mrs. Hardy told him. "The boys will show you. Chet, you're right next door."

They all decided to go up. Ace waved at the Hardy boys before he closed his door. "See you at six for the run?"

"Not me," Chet protested.

Joe laughed. "Chet isn't big on physical exercise early in the morning, but I'll be there."

"Me, too," Frank echoed.

Everybody in the house was asleep within a few minutes, except for Chet. He found that the outside lights which stayed on as a security measure kept him awake.

Suddenly, he heard a whizzing sound and a thud on the roof. Then he smelled smoke! He jumped out of bed and opened the window. "Fire!" he yelled. "The roof's on fire!"

16 No Charge

The first people to hear Chet were Frank and Joe. Joe dashed for a phone while Frank awoke the other sleepers. Ace was the most difficult to wake. Frank half dragged him out of his room before the boy was fully conscious.

"What's going on?" Ace asked. "Is this some kind of game?"

"The roof is on fire," Frank said grimly.

A minute later, fire engines came roaring down the street. Ladders were raised and firemen scampered up. It took a few minutes to douse the flames. Little damage had been done, although there was a gaping hole in the roof.

The fire chief walked over to Fenton Hardy,

who was standing on the grass. "This was no accident." He pointed at a smoldering black mass brought down from the roof. "That caused the fire. It's a greasy cloth ball coated with oil and gas and other inflammable substances we haven't figured out yet."

"A form of Greek fire!" Chet, who was standing near, spoke up. "It was commonly used in the Middle Ages in sieges."

Fenton Hardy looked at the youth with raised eyebrows.

"Chet's new hobby is studying medieval weapons, remember?" Joe put in.

"It wasn't only the Greeks who used it," Chet went on. "Everyone did. It was hard to put out."

"That's right," the fire chief said. "We had to use chemicals because water didn't seem to do any good."

"The Greek fire might be poured on an arrow or an object like that one and hurled by a catapult," Chet explained.

"A catapult, eh?" Fenton Hardy said. He went into the house and returned with a flashlight. Then everyone followed him outside to search the bushes on the other side of the street for evidence. "Here it is!" he suddenly cried out.

They saw a catapult about four feet high, hidden by the greenery.

"That's a good model," Chet said.

"Don't touch it. We'll leave that for the police," Mr. Hardy ordered.

Just then the blue and white police car marked CHIEF came around the corner and stopped by the curb where they were standing.

Chief Collig of the Bayport Police Department got out. "What's been going on, Fenton?"

"We've had a strange kind of arson," Mr. Hardy said and quickly related the events of the evening.

"We'll take the catapult down to headquarters and go over it very carefully," the chief declared. "I'll let you know what we come up with. In the meantime, I'll station an officer to stand guard in front of your house and another in back."

"This firebug was very clever," Mr. Hardy mused as he ushered his family and guests back into the house. "He saw he couldn't get to the house without exposing himself in the light. So he found a way to shoot at us from across the street. I'd like to advise you gentlemen not to talk about this on campus. It might get in the way of an investigation."

Ace was very upset. "No doubt it was another attempt to harm me," he said. "Someone must have followed us when we drove here."

"Go back to bed," Joe said gently. "We'll make sure the rest of the night is peaceful."

The Hardys took turns standing watch, and Ace skipped his morning run. After breakfast, Frank, Joe, Chet, and the young athlete started back to the university. They dropped Chet off at the dorm, then went to the courthouse. They walked into the district attorney's office exactly at nine o'clock. Carol was already sitting there, looking very small, scared, and defiant at the same time. Chief Higgins and the police expert entered and took seats.

The DA, a short, slim man of Oriental origin, whose name was Gilbert Chang, stood up and leaned on his desk with his arms.

"I want everyone to realize that this meeting is being held to see if I should present the case concerning this young lady to a grand jury. There seems to be some doubt as to whether Ms. Crider could have executed this attempt on the life of Mr. Harrington."

"She couldn't," Ace said doggedly.

The official allowed himself a small smile and sat down again. "Unfortunately, your simple denial weighs very little." He turned toward the police expert. "Why do you think she could not have shot the arrow, Sergeant?"

"The attempt was made with a crossbow, Mr.

Chang. That takes a great deal of strength and it seems to me that she does not possess such power."

"I do so," Carol said hotly.

"For Pete's sake, Carol, keep your mouth shut," Ace hissed. "That's no way to get off."

"I don't care. This man may be well-intentioned, but he just doesn't seem to know what women can do. They'll find out sooner or later, anyhow." She turned back to the district attorney. "I've been able to handle a crossbow—in fact, almost any kind of bow—for a long time. Back home in Tennessee, I was a state champion in archery."

Ace groaned and put his head in his hands.

"Your honesty is commendable, Ms. Crider," Mr. Chang said. "I hope you realize that under the circumstances we have no option but to hold you for—"

"There's more, Mr. Chang," the police expert said.

"I'm sorry. I thought you were through. What else?"

"Since Mr. Hardy came up with it, I think he ought to have the honor," the officer said, nodding toward Frank.

Frank carefully explained how Carol's height would make the angle of the arrow impossible.

"The culprit had to be someone six to eight inches taller," he finished.

The district attorney glanced toward the police expert and Chief Higgins. "Do you corroborate all this?"

They nodded.

Mr. Chang smiled and stood up. "In that case, the case is dismissed with apologies to Ms. Crider. If I ever get into trouble, I hope my friends will be as helpful as yours, young lady."

"Thanks," Carol said quietly.

"I also want to remind you all not to talk about the details of the case," the DA concluded before the young people left his office.

"We'll drive you back to campus," Frank told Carol as they walked downstairs.

The young woman was half laughing and half crying. "You're on!" she said and ran back to the district attorney's office, where in her excitement she'd left her bookbag.

While they were waiting, Frank told Chief Higgins about the fire.

"I've been on the force twenty-seven years," the police official said, "and I've never come across a stranger case than this. Thanks for bringing me up to date."

Frank climbed into the driver's seat with Joe next to him, while Ace and Carol sat in the rear.

"I want to thank you all," she said. "Ace, I just don't know why you went to all this trouble to help me, particularly after the cruel things I've said to you. I'm really ashamed of myself."

"Aw, forget it." Ace was embarrassed. "I said some stupid things, too. Anyhow, I wouldn't want anybody to go to jail when they're innocent." He took a breath and added, "Especially you."

"That's nice of you," she said in a small voice. "I hope you know that while I still believe that college sports are given too much importance, I really admire you. You've managed to keep your work and athletics in perspective."

There was a long silence. At last, Ace said, "Say, you must be hungry. How about coming to the student center with me and having something to eat? My next class isn't for an hour."

"I'd like that," she agreed.

"Great! Hey, fellows, stop here, will you? The student center is just down the block."

Frank and Joe watched the couple walk away. "Would you have believed such a thing could happen just a few days ago?" Joe grinned. "There they go, two friendly enemies."

"I would change that to friends," Frank said, smiling. "Come on!" he got out of the car.

"Where are you going?"

"We're still Ace's bodyguards, remember?"

17 *Another Arrow*

The Hardys and Chet spent the rest of the day taking turns searching for Robbie around campus, but without success. They called the police, who had no news either. Disappointed, they resolved to look again the next day. In the meantime, they could feel the excitement of the rally building all around them.

It was the largest one in the history of State University. Old furniture donated by the people of the city, wooden beams, and firewood were piled as high as two stories. A platform had been erected in front of this huge heap.

Ace, Chet, and the Hardy brothers went to the rally location right after supper to see the crowd of students putting the finishing touches on the structure under the watchful eye of the city fire chief and Pops Walzak. They chatted for a few minutes with the head of the campus guards. Ace told him about the roof fire in Bayport the night before.

Pops shook his head. "When will this nonsense end? Last night someone konked our stadium guard and tied him up. We didn't find him until this morning."

"Was anything stolen?" Frank asked.

"That's the strangest thing. Only his keys were missing. We checked over the whole place with a fine-tooth comb and we couldn't spot a thing out of place. Some weirdo, probably."

The rally started at eight o'clock sharp. President Catello, Coach Bradley, the team, and the cheerleaders mounted the platform. Pops Walzak stood in back of them.

The wood was lit and very soon the flames of an enormous bonfire leaped high into the sky. As it blazed, the cheerleaders led the throng in a school song.

"Frank and Joe Hardy, could I speak to you for a few minutes?" Mrs. Stevenson was pulling Frank's sleeve. They and Chet followed her to the edge of the crowd where they could hear each other speak.

"I'm not sure which one of you is Frank and which is Joe," she said.

"I'm Joe. This is Frank and this is our friend Chet Morton."

"I was so agitated the other day that I wasn't listening properly," she said.

"Did you hear from Robbie?" Frank asked eagerly.

She shook her head. In the firelight, they could see her face was drawn, and there were shadows under her eyes. "These past few days have been the worst ones of my life. First Robbie being so brutally beaten and then disappearing. The third blow came yesterday when you came to my office."

"We didn't mean to upset you," Frank said.

"No, no, it was right that I should know."

"Know what?" Joe asked.

"Well, the gold bug you referred to is a story by Edgar Allan Poe. A few months ago, the university was given a very old and rare edition of *The Gold Bug*. It was placed in the library, of course. When I returned from the hospital yesterday, I checked our rare books section. The book was gone! A fake had been put in its place."

"That's what Meeb gave Robbie that night in the basement!" Frank said, snapping his fingers.

The rare books room is kept under lock and key. And I have the only key. I don't know of any person who could have taken that key and the book except Robbie. My poor boy is a thief!" She buried her head in her hands, weeping.

"He did it for you," Frank said gently. "It all fits together now. Meeb and Scrabby, have been bullying Robbie. Worse yet, they have been telling him they will assault you if he didn't do what they said. This apparently convinced him. They gave him the fake book that he exchanged for the real one."

"That was clever," she said, "because not many people look at it. The deception might not have been discovered for weeks, even months."

"And by that time, the real book would have been sold by Meeb for an enormous profit. He probably knows a collector who would have paid him a fortune for it." Frank went on. "Anyhow, Robbie couldn't bring himself to give over the book. Apparently, he's hidden it. That's why they have beaten him up."

"Well, it's a small comfort to know that he didn't give them the book. But where is he now?"

"We've searched the campus thoroughly and he isn't here," Joe put in.

"We don't know," Frank said. "But you're in danger, too, grave danger. Where do you live?"

"Why, in an apartment building on Wilson Street," the startled lady said.

"I think someone should be with you when you go home."

"I'll go," Joe volunteered. "Are you coming, too, Chet?"

"Sure thing."

"I want to go home now," the library director said, "in case Robbie phones."

"When you get there, Joe, check the apartment thoroughly," Frank said. "Then call Chief Higgins and give him the story. Ask him if he would station a guard for the night outside her door."

"Will do."

"I'm truly grateful for this and for your being nice to Robbie. He has an instinct for searching out good people." She sighed. "Tomorrow I'm going to submit my resignation as library director."

"Oh, don't do that," Frank said. "At least, wait for a few days. Everything may be resolved by that time."

She nodded. "I'll wait until Monday."

When they were gone, Frank turned his attention back to the rally. President Catello was the first to speak. He told the team that the entire student body was proud of them, not only for their winning record, but for the sportsmanship they had exhibited all season. He then gave the microphone to Coach Bradley, who started to introduce each of the players.

Frank turned to find Professor Overton, who was standing next to him. "It's something else. I've never seen a rally before. It's going to make the game tomorrow even more exciting."

"You know my views on that," Overton said stiffly. "I, of course, will not be in attendance." He softened a bit as he added, "On the other hand, I wish the team—especially Ace—well. Tell him I'm happy that he was not hit by the quarrel the other night, and that he escaped from last night's fire safely."

"I'm sorry about the International Society of Physicists turning down your bid to speak," Frank said in a lowered voice. He wished he could have taken the words back as soon as he had said them.

Overton clenched his fists. "So they are already spreading the word that they have turned me down? I saw them arriving this afternoon. Of course, they pretended to be nice to me, but I knew what they were thinking, how underneath the facade, they were smirking and making fun of me. I shall not attend the symposium so they can laugh at me more. Scientists they call themselves." He sneered. "Do you know what these so-called world-renowned physicists are going to do tomorrow, Hardy? He held Frank's sleeve and focused his eyes upon the youth in an infuriated stare. "They are actually going to the football game! Serious scholars wasting their time. President Catello invited them. He should have known better. Do you see what kind of people . . . they are? You see why they ignore my findings? Jealousy, pure jealousy! Someday they shall learn what fools they have been . . . and that day will be sooner than later!"

He stumbled away. Frank looked after him with pity in his eyes.

A few minutes later, Joe and Chet returned. "All set," the younger Hardy said. "The chief is sending over a man to Mrs. Stevenson's within an hour. I told her not to open her door until he arrives."

"Fine," Frank said. Then he told them about

his encounter with Professor Overton.

Joe sighed. "Poor guy. He sure needs help."

All the players except one had been introduced by this time, and that one was its star and captain. The students started to yell, "Ace, Ace, Ace!"

The sports star came forward and bedlam reigned throughout the crowd. They whistled, cheered, screamed, and threw hats in the air. Ace raised his hand for silence, but his fans paid no attention. After five minutes, they calmed down and he was able to speak.

"I know I'm talking for Coach Bradley and my teammates when I tell you that we appreciate your support and enthusiasm. You have given us that all season. Tomorrow we really need you. When we hear your cheering in our ears, we'll try that much harder. See you all tomorrow."

A number of the students pulled him off the platform, raised him to their shoulders, and started to parade him through the campus. The crowd melted away, leaving the boys and a few stragglers.

Joe was frowning. Frank looked at him and asked, "What's up?"

"Come on," the younger brother said. He hopped up on the platform. "Everything was happening so fast at the end that I didn't believe my eyes."

"What did you see?" Chet asked.

"Something flying." Joe studied the platform until he reached the spot where Ace had stood. "I was right. There it is. One more tenth of a second and Ace would have been hit."

They followed his stare. There at his feet was another arrow!

At last, Ace rejoined them. He was laughing. "I managed to slip off their shoulders over by the student center. They still wouldn't let me go so I had to run for it. I circled the entire campus. Let's go before they show up again."

As they hurried toward the parking lot, Ace said, "You guys look like you lost your best friend. How come you're so down in the mouth?"

The three youths had decided they would not worry Ace by telling him about the latest attempt on his life.

"No reason at all," Joe said, faking a laugh.

The next day was crisp and cold, a perfect day for a football game. After their six o'clock run, while Ace was still getting dressed, the boys went to a public phone in the dorm and called their father. Quickly, they told him about the mysterious arrow.

"It certainly is strange," Fenton Hardy said. "I still think my theory is correct. Whoever is after him is not a gambler. There's a deeper reason for trying to kill Ace. But he ought to be safe during the game. No one in the stadium is going to stand up and shoot a crossbow or use a catapult to set him on fire. We'll have to talk to President Catello about this latest situation. Stick with Ace until then."

"We will. He has one class and then he has to be at the stadium early," Frank said.

"All right. Your mother and I will leave about noon. See you later."

The morning was uneventful. After Ace's class, the three youths accompanied him to the stadium, where they left him. After that, they strolled across the campus.

"You've been quiet all morning, Frank," Chet observed.

"I've noticed it, too," Joe remarked.

"I don't know. Something is stuck in my mind and won't come out," Frank confessed.

Chet struck him lightly on the back of the head. "That help?"

Frank chuckled. "Not much. It has something to do with words."

"Relax and it will come to you," Joe advised. "Hey, here's President Catello."

The college administrator was smiling broadly. Accompanying him were an attractive woman and a Catholic priest. "Frank and Joe! My dear and Father Ryan, I'd like you to meet two of the smartest young men it has been been my pleasure to meet. May I also introduce Mrs. Catello and Father Thomas Ryan, president of Northern University."

Frank smiled. "I thought the two of you would be deadly enemies."

"Us?" President Catello laughed. "We went to graduate school at Harvard together. We certainly are friendly rivals this afternoon, but there never has and will never be any quarrel between us."

After they had passed, Frank snapped his fingers in excitement, "That's it!" he exclaimed. "He said the word!"

18 The Clincher

"President Catello?" Joe was bewildered. "What did he say?"

Frank was already moving. "Let's go," he shouted. "We don't have much time." He stopped first at a public phone booth to check an address, then he started to run toward the parking lot.

"If I didn't know better," Chet panted, "I would say he's gone crazy."

Frank drove the car. In a few minutes, they pulled up before a small building with the sign: MEDIEVAL CLUB.

"That's the one I was telling you about," Chet cried. "The best one in the state."

Frank jumped out of their sports sedan and ran into the building. By the time Chet and Joe entered, he was talking to a haughty-looking man in the hallway of the club.

"Yes, I am the secretary," the man said, "but I simply cannot permit you to examine our membership list. It's out of the question."

"It's a matter of life or death," Frank said earnestly. "Look, if you won't help us, I will call Police Chief Higgins and he'll come with a search warrant. Make up your mind."

The secretary surrendered. "Oh, very well. Wait here a moment, I'll bring you the list."

When he left, Joe grabbed his brother by the arm. "Would you mind telling us what you're up to?"

"Sure," Frank replied. "Remember when Overton spoke to us in the stadium, he knew Ace had been shot at with a *quarrel?* Yet no one was to mention the fact that the arrow was shot with a crossbow, and I don't think anyone did."

"You're right!" Joe cried. "And you know what else just occurred to me? Overton talked about the Bayport fire. How did he know about that? Even if it was in the newspaper at home, I doubt he reads the Bayport papers."

Just then the man reappeared with a large

ledger. Frank opened it and scanned the present membership list until his finger stopped at a familiar name—*Geoffrey C. Overton*.

Frank, Joe, and Chet thanked the secretary and ran out to the car. Ten minutes later, they had returned to campus. They sprinted to the science building and took the steps three at a time until they reached Professor Overton's office on the third floor. They burst through the door.

The scientist was sitting at his desk, examining a large sheet of paper. He looked up at them with a benign expression. "Hello, there. How nice of you to drop in. I thought you would be at the football game by now. What can I do for you?"

Frank glared at him. "Professor Overton, why did you try to kill Ace with a crossbow and use a fireball to try to burn down our house?"

Overton smiled broadly. "If you were a student, I would say that you have been studying too hard and need a rest. What on earth gave you such a fantastic notion, Frank?"

"You did," the older Hardy said. "You gave yourself away last night."

"And just how did I do that?" Overton asked in a gentle tone of voice as if he were talking to a child.

"You mentioned that the arrow Ace had been

attacked with was a quarrel, which means it was shot with a crossbow. Yet no one on campus knew that."

"And you happen to know how to handle a crossbow," Chet added, "since you practice at the Medieval Club!"

"Where you stole one of their model catapults so you could shoot a cloth ball doused with Greek fire substances onto our roof in Bayport!" Frank went on relentlessly. "You were the only person who knew we had taken Ace home with us that night besides Dr. Catello."

Overton was standing stock-still, his face ashen. "The clincher," he murmured. "That's the clincher."

"Right!" Frank said. "But we don't understand your motive. You told us Ace was your prize pupil. And he admires you immensely and looks upon you almost as a father. Did you bet heavily on Northern?"

The question made Overton laugh almost hysterically. "Do you think that I, one of the greatest scientific minds in the world, care two cents about that silly game? My prize pupil? Of course, he is. But I created a monster!"

Frank was bewildered. "I don't get it. What are you talking about?"

Overton pointed his shaking finger at him.

"You were here when it happened. He found the formula! It was the missing link of how to extract oil from shale cheaply! I developed the entire process except for that. After the many years that I have spent searching for it! And this young upstart, this athletic genius comes up with it in one class period! And the irony of the whole thing is that he doesn't know what he found. He doesn't know! He thinks it's just a minor part of an enormous system! I knew what it was the moment I looked at it."

Overton had a fit of simultaneous laughter and weeping. "And he never will know what he has done!" he cried. "He won't live long enough to find out. Nor will Catello and those stuck-up physicists who have snubbed me so long!"

With that, he ran to the open window, and before either of the boys could reach him, leaped out nimbly onto a ledge and moved toward a fire escape in the center of the building.

Joe went after him. "I'll get him!" he shouted. "You call the police!" Frank, however, did not have to put through the call. Pops Walzak and two of his men were walking toward the stadium when they heard Joe yell and looked up. The campus police chief didn't know what was going on, but he immediately ordered his men to stand at the bottom of the fire escape while he went upstairs.

Frank and Chet watched anxiously as Joe gained on the scientist. "Get away, get away!" Overton shrieked. "Get away or I'll hurt you!"

He tried to open windows as he passed, but all were locked. When Joe put his hand on the professor's shoulder, Overton screamed and pushed the young man violently. Joe lost his footing and almost fell off, but managed to recover his balance at the last moment.

The professor slipped a moment later and started to fall, but clung to the ledge with his fingertips. Joe reached him as Overton's strength was almost exhausted and pulled him up. With no strength left, the professor meekly allowed himself to be guided down the fire escape.

"Bring him back here to the office," Pops Walzak called to his men after hearing what had happened from Frank.

As they escorted Overton through the building, his mouth hung open and his eyes stared out into endless space. He hummed the same tune over and over again.

"He's flipped," Pops said. "You say that he mentioned Ace wouldn't live long. What did he mean by that?"

Frank shook his head in frustration. "I don't know."

Overton came back to reality for a moment. "And you never will know," he screamed, "until it is too late!" Then he went back into his comatose state.

"I know," a voice suddenly came from inside the closet. To everyone's consternation, the door opened and out stepped Robbie Stevenson!

"Robbie!" Joe shouted. "Where have you been?"

"I've been hiding in the science building so Scrabby couldn't find me. Professor Overton rarely goes out for lunch and there's always food in the place. No one knew I was here, not even the night watchman. Anyway, I've been in the closet all morning watching the professor. He's been acting real funny."

"In what way?" Frank asked.

"He's been looking at that sheet on his desk and giggling and laughing."

Frank and Pops looked at the paper. "It's a map of the stadium," Walzak said.

"What do these X's mean, though?" Joe asked. "Look, they're all over—six on each side of the stadium and one in the locker room area."

"He was talking to himself while I was in the

closet," Robbie said, "about things going boom at one o'clock sharp."

"Explosives!" Frank exclaimed. "We've got to get down there!"

"You keep watching this guy," Pops told his two men. Then he yelled after Frank, "I'll phone the stadium and then catch up to you." Then he said to himself, "I hope I'm lucky. They are always too busy to answer at this time."

The four youths tore down the hill toward the stadium. Frank glanced at his watch. Twenty-five minutes to one! Only twenty-five minutes until the bombs would go off!

19 Chaos

The four youths reached the gate. The ticket-
taker casually put out his hand for tickets, but
Frank barged past him. When the man turned
with his mouth open to stare after Frank, the
other three rushed past him, too.

The attendant finally found his voice. "Hey,
stop there! You haven't got tickets!"

The stadium was horseshoe-shaped. Frank
circled around to the open end of the horse-
shoe-shape evading ushers who heard the
ticket-taker's shout. Ace would have been
proud of him. The older Hardy ran like a star
back through the secondary defense.

An ambulance was parked at the open end so

that if any player was seriously hurt, he could be rushed to the hospital. At the moment, the ambulance was empty. Frank leaped into it and started the engine. "Joe, hop in!" he said as the others came up. "Chet, get on top and yell for people to get out of the stadium."

He dared not take the time to wait for Robbie, who had been lagging behind. But the youth had found a bike and was coming up fast.

The ambulance swung out onto the track that surrounded the field. It started around slowly so that the spectators could hear Chet yelling.

When it arrived in front of President Catello's box, Frank said to Joe, "You take over." Then he leaped out as Joe grabbed the wheel. Frank jumped the fence that separated the stands from the field and ran up the steps leading to the president's box.

"What's the meaning of this, Frank?" The administrator's face was a mixture of confusion and anger. "The game's about to—"

"No time to explain," Frank said. "Explosives are set to go off at one. We must get people out."

Catello rose immediately. "Yes, yes, of course. But how?"

"If you get on the PA system, you can tell the crowd," Frank panted.

The college president and Frank started running toward the broadcasters' booth. In a minute, Catello's voice boomed throughout the stadium. "Ladies and gentlemen, please listen very carefully to what I am saying. It's extremely important. It is necessary that we all leave the stadium at once. Please do not panic. Take the most convenient exit—that is, the one that is nearest to you. Those people in the south end of the field can go out through the open end of the stadium. All ushers, guards, and attendants will help you to evacuate in a safe and orderly manner. Please go as far away from the field as possible."

Joe and Chet were still circling the arena in the ambulance, repeating the president's message. Robbie made the circuit in the opposite direction, shouting directions. He rode right into the midst of the Northern University team, which had been doing warm-ups. The players were in a state of confusion after Catello had spoken, uncertain if the message was also directed at them. Robbie hastily called out instructions and they started going toward the open end of the field.

The crowd left in an orderly fashion. There was no hysteria or pushing or running, only bewilderment and curiosity at this strange turn of events.

Frank suddenly clapped his hand to his forehead. "Our team is still in the locker room! They took their warm-ups and went back in for a pep talk by Coach Bradley!"

"They can't hear the PA in there," Catello groaned. "They'll be killed!"

"Not if I can help it!" Frank exclaimed. He flew down the steps three at a clip and sprinted across the field. At the same time, he waved to Joe, Chet, and Robbie to get out of the stadium.

The clock said three minutes to one when Frank burst through the door to the locker room. "Get out!" he shouted.

The team was sitting on benches. Coach Bradley faced them, drawing a diagram on a blackboard. Everybody stared at Frank in surprise, but no one moved.

Frank yelled his warning again. Then Ace acted. "If he says go, we go!" He led the way out of the back door.

Frank was trying to catch up to the football star when they were leaving the stadium. It was then that he got a fleeting glance of Scrabby and Meeb in the crowd ahead of them.

I hope they don't see Robbie! Frank thought fervently as he managed to move alongside of Ace.

"What's all this about?" the football star asked him.

Frank was about ready to drop from exhaustion, but he managed to gasp, "The stadium is going to blow up!"

One minute later, there was an earth-shattering explosion!

Huge chunks of concrete rose straight into the air and rained down on the stadium. None flew out of the massive oval. One part of the stands fell with an enormous roar, creating a gray dust cloud that hung over the playing field.

"There must have been a charge against a support pillar," Ace called out over his shoulder.

In some places the dust cloud was thin, and the immobilized crowd stared at the scene that looked like a moonscape—a lifeless picture of rocks and holes. It was hard to believe that they had been in there only a few minutes before, happily cheering and joking. People spoke in whispers and in awe.

Frank and Ace met up with Joe and Chet. They suddenly spotted Mr. Hardy in the crowd. He waved and made his way over to the group.

"Mother and Aunt Gertrude are further up," he explained. "What's going on?"

Frank quickly told him how they had figured out Professor Overton's plan to blow up the stadium.

"He did all that to get rid of Ace?" The detective whistled. "It seems rather drastic."

"He also wanted to kill the physicists who snubbed him, Dad," Frank said and explained what had happened.

"Ingenious. When did you first suspect Overton?"

"When he mentioned the quarrel. Of course, I didn't *really* know whether word about the crossbow had somehow leaked out. So I just confronted him, and he admitted everything."

"So the mystery is cleared up."

"Well, *that* mystery is cleared up. But another one is still open, although I think it's about to be resolved." Frank looked around. "We'll have to find our friend Robbie."

"I told him about meeting with his mother, and that she's at home under guard. I also told him that she knows about the book," Joe said.

"So where is he?"

"He's on his way home. He said he wanted to explain things to his mother."

"Why did you let him do that?" Frank cried in alarm. "Meeb and Scrabby are still at large. I saw them a little while ago!"

"But it's daylight," Joe retorted, "and there are thousands of people around."

"The thousands are around here, Joe," Frank said.

Frank waved to the group, "Come on!" He started the long, gradual hill to the north campus.

As much as he wished to sprint, Frank's legs were too tired to keep pace with Chet and Joe, who passed him. Nor could Ace with his football uniform on do much better than run side by side with Frank. Slightly behind them came Mr. Hardy.

As Frank feared, the upper part of the campus was practically deserted. He set his lips tightly. If only they could reach Robbie in time before Scrabby and Meeb waylaid him!

"I see him," Joe called back and pointed. A small figure was still a good distance ahead of them, but he had Robbie's distinctive gait. Joe yelled for him to stop, but his voice was lost in the wind and Robbie continued on.

Suddenly, from behind a tree came Scrabby and Meeb!

20 *Capture*

Joe and Chet dashed ahead as fast as they could. Scrabby seized Robbie's arm and the youth sunk to his knees in excruciating pain.

"Where is the book?" Meeb screamed. "Tell me where it is or Scrabby will rip your arm off!"

Then Chet and Joe arrived. Chet jumped on Scrabby's back. The giant roared like a bull and his grip eased enough for Joe to pull Robbie away.

Meeb charged at the young boy, but Robbie easily moved out of his way, causing his attacker to trip and fall.

Scrabby tried to shake Chet off his back, grabbing for the youth with his gigantic hands.

But Chet was clinging tightly to his neck. Scrabby adopted another strategy—he bent over and jumped up and down. Still Chet held on.

Joe rushed at their adversary. He kicked at Scrabby's ankle in the style of a football field-goal kicker. Scrabby howled and aimed a mighty blow at Joe, but the younger Hardy ducked and kicked again, this time hitting the other ankle.

Scrabby fell like a tall tree, and Chet scrambled off. By this time, Frank and Ace had came up. They pounced on Scrabby.

The huge man put up his arms to protect his face. "Don't hit me," he whimpered. "Don't hit me no more."

Fenton Hardy arrived. He took off his belt and used it to bind Scrabby's wrists.

Just then everyone noticed Meeb starting to run away.

"Stop him!" Frank yelled.

Joe and Robbie chased the small thug. Meeb had only taken a few steps when the youth he had tormented grabbed his leg and held on tightly.

"I've got him, Joe, I've got him!" Robbie cried out jubilantly.

"You sure do," Joe said as he grabbed the

dazed crook. "That was beautiful. Ace couldn't have done it better!"

The group marched the two criminals to Main Street, where they found a police officer. He called in to headquarters, and a few minutes later they were all in a paddy wagon. Chief Higgins met them and was delighted to see that Scrabby and Meeb were being charged with assault, forcing a minor to commit an unlawful act, and a number of other felonies they had committed in the past.

"That was some explosion at the stadium," he said. "I've just returned, but practically my entire force is still down there plus thirty state troopers. Ace, Professor Overton sure must have had it in for you. We got into the locker room and it was some mess. The charge went off in a locker that Coach Bradley identified as yours."

"I lost my new sportscoat," the football star said mournfully, then brightened. "But I'm alive to buy another one!"

"Is anyone hurt?" Fenton Hardy inquired.

"Not a soul," Chief Higgins said. "It's a miracle. Thousands of people and not one person injured. Your sons really did a great job!"

They were returned to the campus in the paddy wagon, which amused Mr. Hardy. "I hope anyone who sees us knows we're not on our way to jail. But, after all, we couldn't all fit into one patrol car with a driver."

"Now we just have to clear up one thing yet," Frank said. "Robbie, where'd you leave *The Gold Bug*?"

"In your room." The boy grinned.

"What? In our room?" Joe was incredulous. "You have to be joking."

Robbie chuckled. "Sorry, but I can't think of any jokes right now."

"I'm not surprised," Joe said. "But where *did* you hide the book?"

"I'll show you," Robbie said eagerly. "You'll laugh."

They went to the boys' old dorm room. Robbie immediately headed for a bookshelf near the window. He took out a slim volume and handed it to Joe. "Here it is."

Joe held the book very gingerly for fear that it would fall apart. "And all that trouble Meeb and Scrabby went to for this!"

"I'll tell you what, Robbie," Mr. Hardy said. "After Ace changes his clothes, we'll all drive over to your apartment and you can give this to your mother."

"I hope she's not mad at me," Robbie said anxiously. "I did do the right thing in the end, didn't I?"

The detective smiled. "You did just fine,

Robbie, just fine." He patted him on the back. "That was a very clever move, hiding a book among other books. Who would have thought of looking there?"

"Not Meeb and Scrabby, anyhow," Frank added.

Two weeks later, President Catello held a party to celebrate the team's successful season. The Hardys, Chet, Robbie and his mother, the faculty, the athletic staff, and, of course, the team were at the president's house for the occasion.

President and Mrs. Catello took the Hardy family on a tour of the old colonial house that was the home of all State University presidents. Then the college head asked them to come into his private study.

"I thought you would be interested in what happened to Professor Overton. A team of psychiatrists appointed by a judge have examined him to see if he was sane enough to stand trial for his crimes. Their unanimous decision was that he committed them when he was deranged, his sanity destroyed by his obsessive and unceasing work on his oil extraction project."

"I'm glad," Fenton Hardy said. "It's also fortunate that he didn't do more damage than he did."

"Well, he did burn a hole in our roof," Mrs. Hardy pointed out.

"And almost destroyed an entire stadium," Aunt Gertrude sniffed.

"What I meant was that he didn't injure anyone except that poor stadium guard he knocked out so that he could set his explosives without being disturbed," Mr. Hardy explained.

"And the guard, thank heaven, is all right," President Catello continued. "As for the stadium, I can't even count how many local contractors came forward to volunteer their services and provide crews. They worked on a round-the-clock basis so that the stadium was repaired within a few days. Otherwise, we never would have been able to play the game the following Saturday, perhaps not at all this season."

"It's too bad State didn't win," Joe said.

President Catello winked. "I'm not devastated by the 14-14 tie. I rejoice that both my friend Father Ryan and I can say that our institutions enjoyed undefeated seasons." He chuckled. "However, I do hope that my little confession will not go beyond the walls of this room. I wouldn't like Coach Bradley or Ace

Harrington to hear it. Oh, by the way, speaking of Ace, Mrs. Stevenson and Robbie have asked if his brother Bill can stay with them. We have applied to state authorities for permission, and they have agreed. So there is another problem solved."

"I just can't get over how Professor Overton turned against Ace," Frank said. "He seemed to like him very much."

"Apparently, he was very fond of him," President Catello said. "However, that was all swept aside when Ace came up unwittingly with the new formula for extracting oil from shale. That, coupled with the refusal of the International Society of Physicists to hear him, unhinged his mind."

"It's a shame that such a smart man will be locked up forever, never again to teach or practice science," Mrs. Catello said sadly.

"Perhaps not," her husband said. "The psychiatrists say that with treatment over a period of years, there is an excellent chance he may recover his sanity." He rose. "I think Mrs. Catello and I had better return to mingle with our guests."

As they walked downstairs, the college president said, "Did you hear that Ace has insisted that Overton get credit for the formula Ace discovered?"

"No, we haven't had a chance to talk to him," Frank said. "We went back to home after the game and haven't seen Ace until tonight."

Catello went on, "His justification for doing this is that he never would have stumbled on the formula if Overton hadn't assigned him to the project, and that the professor taught him a great deal. His decision to become a physicist was largely influenced by Overton."

"That's a very generous gesture on Ace's part," Joe said, impressed.

"Yes. It is a testament of his fine character," Dr. Catello agreed.

The boys went downstairs, wondering on the way if there would be another mystery for them to solve. They had no idea that soon they would be involved in *The Crimson Flame*.

When the boys arrived downstairs, they saw Mrs. Hardy and Aunt Gertrude at the cake table, while Mr. Hardy was talking to one of the faculty. They wandered out to the patio where they found Bill Harrington and Robbie throwing a football to each other on the lawn. Mrs. Stevenson was watching them.

"We heard Bill's going to live with you," Frank said to the woman. "It was very nice of you to offer this arrangement."

Her eyes twinkled. "It's not as unselfish as it appears. The two of them seem fond of each other, and I think Robbie has been lonely. Also, Bill likes to be near his older brother."

"You must feel a lot safer now that Meeb and Scrabby are in jail," Joe put in.

"Oh, I do. And I'm glad Robbie won't be charged, since they forced him to steal the book."

"How're you doing, guys?" Ace called to them from a corner of the room where he was sitting with Carol Crider.

"We're doing fine, Ace," Frank replied. "That was some game you played against Northern."

Just then Chet walked up to the brothers. "Guess where their next game is," he said.

"Where?" Joe asked.

"Tell him, Ace." Chet grinned.

"It's a bowl game in Memphis, Tennessee," Ace replied. "The day before New Year's Eve. And guess who lives in Memphis?"

"Who?"

"Carol. Since school will be out for winter vacation then, her parents have invited Bill and me to stay with them. And—best of all—she's overcome her prejudices and will be at the game!"

"Wow!" Frank exclaimed. "That's some news! You'll have a wonderful vacation!"

The athlete smiled broadly. "Yes sir, that's what it'll be, a *very* nice vacation."

OVER THREE MILLION PAPERBACKS SOLD IN FIVE YEARS!
WHICH OF THESE MYSTERY BOOKS ARE YOU
MISSING FROM YOUR COLLECTION?

NANCY DREW® MYSTERY STORIES
By Carolyn Keene

	ORDER NO.	PRICE	QUANTITY
THE TRIPLE HOAX—#57	64278	$3.50	
THE FLYING SAUCER MYSTERY—#58	95601	$3.50	
THE SECRET IN THE OLD LACE—#59	63822	$3.50	
THE GREEK SYMBOL MYSTERY—#60	63891	$3.50	
THE SWAMI'S RING—#61	62467	$3.50	
THE KACHINA DOLL MYSTERY—#62	62474	$3.50	
THE TWIN DILEMMA—#63	62473	$3.50	
CAPTIVE WITNESS—#64	62469	$3.50	
MYSTERY OF THE WINGED LION—#65	62472	$3.50	
RACE AGAINST TIME—#66	62476	$3.50	
THE SINISTER OMEN—#67	62471	$3.50	
THE ELUSIVE HEIRESS—#68	62478	$3.50	
CLUE IN THE ANCIENT DISGUISE—#69	64279	$3.50	
THE BROKEN ANCHOR—#70	62481	$3.50	
THE SILVER COBWEB—#71	62470	$3.50	
THE HAUNTED CAROUSEL—#72	47555	$3.50	
ENEMY MATCH—#73	49735	$3.50	
MYSTERIOUS IMAGE—#74	49737	$3.50	
THE EMERALD-EYED CAT MYSTERY—#75	64282	$3.50	
THE ESKIMO'S SECRET—#76	62468	$3.50	
THE BLUEBEARD ROOM—#77	48743	$3.50	
THE PHANTOM OF VENICE—#78	49745	$3.50	
THE DOUBLE HORROR OF FENLEY PLACE—#79	64387	$3.50	
NANCY DREW®/THE HARDY BOYS®			
BE A DETECTIVE™ MYSTERY STORIES:			
THE FEATHERED SERPENT—#3	49921	$3.50	
SECRET CARGO—#4	49922	$3.50	
NANCY DREW® AND THE HARDY BOYS®			
CAMP FIRE STORIES	50198	$3.50	
NANCY DREW® GHOST STORIES—#1	46468	$3.50	
NANCY DREW® GHOST STORIES—#2	55070	$3.50	
NANCY DREW® AND THE HARDY BOYS® SUPER SLEUTHS	43375	$3.50	
NANCY DREW® AND THE HARDY BOYS® SUPER SLEUTHS #2	50194	$3.50	

and don't forget...THE HARDY BOYS® Now available in paperback

NANCY DREW® and THE HARDY BOYS® are trademarks of Simon & Schuster,
registered in the United States Patent and Trademark Office.

YOU WON'T HAVE A CLUE WHAT YOU'RE MISSING...UNTIL
YOU ORDER. NO RISK OFFER—RETURN ENTIRE PAGE TODAY

Simon & Schuster, Mail Order Dept. ND5
200 Old Tappan Road, Old Tappan, NJ 07675
Please send me copies of the books checked. (If not completely satisfied, return for full refund in 14 days.)

☐ Enclosed full amount per copy with this coupon
(Send check or money order only.)
Please be sure to include proper postage and handling:
95¢—first copy
50¢—each additonal copy ordered.

☐ If order is for $10.00 or more,
you may charge to one of the
following accounts:
☐ Mastercard ☐ Visa

Name _____ Credit Card No. _____

Address _____

City _____ Card Expiration Date _____

State _____ Zip _____ Signature _____

Books listed are also available at your local bookstore. Prices are subject to change without notice.

NDD-02